THE HUNGRY GIRLS

THE HUNGRY GIRLS
And Other Stories

PATRICIA EAKINS

Tough Poets Press
Arlington, Massachusetts

For my mother and father
who have made their peace
with so many mysteries, and
for Peter, my heart's delight

"I give you here the flora and fauna of all the continents, beasts and vegetables, birds and fish, I have seen myself and heard reported. Mind there are many wonders under the sun. Which are God's creations? Which are men's? The truth is not always the likeliest story; thus I credit any careful account."

— Jean Louis Le Montal, in the
foreword of his *Encyclopedia*

"... if we take the ages into our account, may there not be civilization going on among brutes as well as men?"

— Thoreau

CONTENTS

INTRODUCTION

In the long ago when I wrote these stories, I was disturbed by the belief many seemed to hold that animals have no conscious life and no feelings. I had only to look at my cat to know that was not true. I was a firm believer in a continuum of consciousness, and the stories reflect that. Now that the book is about to be republished, anyone can see that it will be reborn into a very different era. It has become commonplace to believe that animals think and feel and have their being on a continuum with our own. Many believe that the future of the planet as a habitable domain depends on human understanding that we share our earthly home with other creatures as equals. For these readers, the challenge to concepts such as "dominion" and "stewardship" represented in *The Hungry Girls* will be reassuring.

With a worldwide rise in literal-minded fundamentalism, the relativity of religions reflected in the stories is less commonplace than it was thirty years ago—though not, perhaps, among my likely readers. Yet nowadays, when people of all religious and political persuasions are tempted to see the world in terms of clear-cut moral categories, the ambiguity of my stories may seem even more alien and threatening than it did in 1989. At that time, the headline writer for Jonathan Baumbach's review of the collection in *The New York Times Book Review* chose the title "Amorality on the Rampage," confident, I assume, of resonance with his well-educated readers. Then as now, it had punk cachet. If only we had put it on tee-shirts!

If good prevails over evil in the stories, it is barely. The grave and the reverent are folded in with the ribald and the mischievous. The fantastic and the fabulous are mingled with the faux-documentary. In 2019, when memoir has supplanted fiction as the dominant literary genre, some readers may bring to the stories an expectation of greater earnestness than they will find here.

In the current marketplace of ideas, I may be accused of appropriating other cultures—though all the cultures I write about are imaginary ones. Thirty years ago, I thought that the imaginary aspect would free me to write as I pleased—to go where I pleased. The book represented a multiplicity of journeys the straitened circumstances of my life as a freelancer and an adjunct did not permit me to take. It seems old-fashioned now, like the journeys of nineteenth-century adventurer-travelers. What remains fresh—even for me—is a Darwinesque curiosity about other lives of all kinds.

I am grateful that Tough Poets Press has snatched my stories from the oubliette of history. Even though the animal and human cultures are imaginary, an elegiac aura hovers over them. In the great extinction in which we find ourselves, all animals are becoming imaginary. And, as the monoculture extends its corporate tentacles into obscure human outposts, the variety of human cultures upon which my stories draw is also becoming imaginary. So, delighted as I am with the gift of recuperation that I have been given thanks to Tough Poets Press and Rick Schober, I am deeply saddened to think that my stories now memorialize vanishing.

Patricia Eakins
5 November 2019

THE HUNGRY GIRLS

The people of Houviers poked each other in the ribs when they first saw the young of the dirt lice burst from their mothers' bodies. The pharmacist had already been watching through the lenses of his shiny new microscope. He claimed the lice sons mate with their sisters even inside the mothers' bodies, then are eaten as the daughters eat their way out.

"Your young will eat anything; one must watch," laughed a townswoman.

"Certainly, Old Cabbage," said another. "And the existence of these *poux de terre*"—these dirt lice—"explains in a modern way our own dirt-eating daughters."

The townspeople claimed they had suspected all along. There had to be something in the soil the human girls had eaten. But did that mean sensible people should walk, in fear of ground, on stilts?

"Go to Father," shrugged the pharmacist.

Long before, when they had all been younger, Father Sempier had convinced with homilies on "earth that crawls with lust," but now the hungry girls were dead, so what was the harm in nibbling a speck of dirt once again? Some of the oldest people recommended the practice; times had been bad before and might get bad again. No use thinking your portion would always be duck with mustard sauce.

Yet the discovery of the dirt lice inspired the priest to new heights of excoriation.

"Father's been nipping Calvados on the sly," said the woman who washed the altar cloths. Indeed the carved confession box had become so fumy some of the parishioners had stopped confessing altogether, maintaining their sins would wait. They consoled themselves with snacks of dirt, joking about the tastiness of the wicked lice.

Even so, prudent people nodded their heads solemnly when the priest fulminated against the miniscule creatures the townspeople had now seen clearly under the pharmacist's microscope.

"Better eat only holy wafers," said the dotards who sat around the fountain in the square. "At the least boil your meat well."

Old Bostiac, the pharmacist, might have charged a few sous for peering into his microscope at the soil, but instead, to spare his white hands and clean shirt, he taught the townspeople to prepare slides.

And the rumor that now and then he popped a crumb of soil in his mouth? Really, it is shameful to recount it. The pharmacist was a man of science, living in Houviers proper, and the truly benighted dirt-eaters, the hungry girls and those whom they seduced, had been mostly ignorant peasants living in the village of La Bouchoire.

On a farm outside La Bouchoire lived Mathilde Sabot, the mother of the first hungry girl. In 1846—otherwise a good year, thanks to Louis Philippe—there was no rain, so no wheat and no potatoes, and Mathilde Sabot, like so many others too proud to seek charity, ate the thatch of her roof, then ate dirt. Later it was said her Jeanne was not born but gnawed her way from Mathilde's stomach, as if a rat had bitten her from within. Mathilde Sabot would have died if Couviard, the horse doctor, had not smelled her blood from the road, doused the hole with carbolic acid, and sewed her up with sheep gut.

When Couviard came into Houviers for his weekly game of Patience with Bostiac, he professed his astonishment. "*Imaginez!* A human baby born with teeth! Poor girl. She was already looking for good things to eat."

By the time Couviard had sewed up Mathilde, Jeanne had caught a starving rat by the tail and was biting off its head, but Couviard did not mention that to Bostiac lest he ruin the Sabots' reputation. Besides, though he was young, he had been long enough among animals to have forgotten the ways of people. Even as he had been trying to sort out what was proper, Jeanne had finished off the rat and climbed into her mother's lap.

"Ah well, the lass has tender feelings after all," the doctor had muttered. Packing his bag, he had been relieved to let it go at that.

By chance no other women in or around La Bouchoire were pregnant that year. So, though many ate dirt, only Mathilde Sabot gave birth to a baby through a hole in her stomach. It was just as well, for Jeanne kept the village busy. When good years followed the bad, and the householders again kept hens, Mathilde's child was forever wringing their necks and eating them.

"A good egg-layer like Madame Rostiard's Froumelle," Mathilde would say to Jeanne, wagging her finger fiercely.

The child would only smile. She said not a word—in fact, she never learned to talk, though she could hum a tune.

Mère de Dieu. Neither Mathilde nor her husband, Robert, knew what to think. Jeanne was large and round, with thick, powerful arms and legs and a huge head, while both the parents were thin and bony, with concave chests, scrawny limbs and small heads.

"You ought to stop that child eating dirt," said the neighbors, who had long since hidden their hens, but Mathilde only shrugged. The child had devoured most of the rats around the village, and many of the cats and dogs. Mathilde could not send her on an errand lest she get at piglets and calves. Only geese, hissing and flapping their powerful wings, sent the enormous toddler waddling away hungry and red-faced, screaming frustration.

When Jeanne was older, the villagers began missing a grandmother's lace, a great-aunt's teapot, even homely, useful objects—a teakettle, a flatiron, a bedwarmer. Of course the villagers suspected Jeanne, but no one could find anything in the Sabots' house or yard, though Mathilde and Robert looked everywhere, digging holes all around their property. *Mère de Dieu!* They shook their daughter and yelled at her, to no avail. Finally the villagers decided the thieves could just as well be outsiders. A new road now ran from Rouen to Houviers, and doubtless remnant Jacobin riff-raff were wandering off it, looking for adventure and trouble.

Still there were whisperings about Jeanne, rumors about what went on in the woods on moonless nights. Everyone knew the enormous girl slept outside. And many a wife woke to find her husband was not in his bed. He would return toward dawn, wet and dirty, claiming he had been to the privy. *Mère de Dieu!* The women began spitting at Jeanne when they passed the eight-year-old with her *maman* buying a paper of pins or length of cloth.

Mathilde then prevailed on Robert to sell the farm and move to another in a remote corner of the parish. Yet though passers-by snickered at the great clumsy barefooted girl, the Sabots themselves were fond of her. At the age of nine, she took over the plowing from her father, driving straight and hard behind the ox, plowing in one day as much as her father could in a week. By the age of twelve she could plow without the ox, though her parents did not like her to do it, lest the neighbors gawk. Of course the parents would have sent her to school, but that was impossible. Mathilde and Robert had taught Jeanne to comb her hair and brush her teeth, and she had learned to cross her ankles when sitting, but they had not been able to housebreak her, so she pissed hot streams and laid steaming cakes of dung wherever she pleased. Her parents cured the dung for fuel and fertilizer, and the Sabot farm began to prosper.

Imagine the grief of the parents to find one evening their useful daughter flat on her back in the fields, the ox having wandered off with the plow. The young woman's body had been gnawed open, and a number of babies were crawling around her. Sabot slid on his shoes and ran all the way to Houviers, interrupting Couviard at his game, while Mathilde did what she could to make her daughter comfortable, stuffing the hole with a pillow and bathing the girl's head with mustard water. Too late.

The doctor advised the parents to gather up the infants crawling about the fields eating dirt and mice. He would examine them to make sure they had been born healthy. And while the grandparents were catching the babies, tying their ankles together and laying them down in a long, empty trough where cattle had drunk, Doctor Couviard began feeling around inside Jeanne, to see if any babies remained. And indeed, one young lady bit his finger—no surprise to the doctor, though he was amazed to find in Jeanne's body cavity no internal organs, only a great many objects—including a Sevres porcelain clock the doctor recognized as his own and a number of little pots he had last seen filled with custard at Madame Hussier's.

"So! We have here the corpse of a thieving stuffcakes," the doctor allowed, smiling and shaking his head. "A greedy fatkin!"

Mathilde and Robert Sabot could not stop wringing their hands and shaking their heads when they saw the pile of objects Doctor Couviard was pulling from their daughter's body. They were all for giving them back at once.

"The andirons of Madame the Baker's great-great-grand-father! The embroidery frame of Father Sempier's housekeeper! And here is the pharmacist's boot-scraper!"

There was a large pile of unidentified objects, and Couviard feared there might be wrangles over these. He suggested that the Sabots sell all the objects; they could then use the money to raise the dozen babies writhing in the watering trough.

And so Sabot loaded onto his haywagon flour sacks containing all the objects except Couviard's clock. These he hauled on the little-used "old road" far past Houviers to the town of Anse-le-Marteau, where he sold them to a dealer in second-hand goods. The money he took in coins which he tied in a sock and tucked inside his blouse. When he got home, he gave most of the coins to his baby granddaughters to see what would happen. And sure enough, they swallowed some and stuffed others into their nostrils, ears, and the holes between their legs.

"This is safer than a bank," he said. "Now we must only wait until they give birth, then we can put our hands in their bellies and take out the coins and whatever else they have stuffed inside. We will want for nothing the rest of our lives, though we must continue to farm for appearances' sake."

With the coins he had not given his granddaughters, Sabot invested in a great deal of seed and a dozen plows. He sold his ox and trained the girls to plow, having rented fields from the larger landowner in the fat thumb of whose holdings Sabot's farm was a sliver.

The girls worked hard and did not fight among themselves as long as each was allowed her field. Robert kept them apart and fed them from separate boxes—hay and apples and dirt—and built a long shed with twelve stalls and a plank roof so the girls could find shelter from rain. At harvest time, he chained them to trees while he took to market what he did not keep for winter feed. One of the chained girls ate straight down past the roots of trees and buried herself alive, but the others waited patiently, only nibbling pits around themselves which, upon unchaining the girls, Robert filled with turnips, potatoes, and sand—his root cellars.

Robert no longer worried what people would think of the hungry girls, who were growing even larger and rounder than Jeanne had. With the profits of his farming, and, eventually, the sale of the loot in the bellies of eleven spent granddaughters, he rented more fields and built more feed-boxes and sheds—enough for 132 great-granddaughters! But he was old by then, and tired of farming and of girls, so he spread word of dowries. With these handsome sums, the girls could actually get husbands, for it seems men who had been frequenting the hungry girls in the forests at night would just as soon marry them by day if there were profit in it. And there was nothing the decent girls of the parish could do but join the convent or go to Paris to work as domestics or whores.

Soon every family in La Bouchoire had a hungry girl for a daughter-in-law, and the same was true in Lamouset, Brosse-les-Bains and Dix-Poulets. Even in Houviers, where the men were used to girls who wore shoes every day, not all the families turned up their noses at the Sabots. But of course it did not work out completely well, for the girls were thieving gluttons who upon dying left their husbands with thieving, gluttonous children—all girls who would require dowries. Then too, not every family in the parish had relied on Doctor Couviard. Most thought themselves too good for an animal man and called on the midwife, Chretienne Lavabo, or the physician, Doctor Nevers; these families did not do well with the hungry brides. Chretienne Lavabo disentombed an ancient Gallic decree declaring a midwife entitled to keep any goods or chattel she pulled from a mother. Dr. Nevers called in the gendarmes, who arrested whole families and accused them of killing the pregnant daughters-in-law by stuffing them with stolen goods. Townspeople were mortified, but in villages like La Bouchoire, they drew a different moral from the events that had passed.

"Couviard's the only decent doctor," they said. And from then on they called on him with all their ailments, especially their births. They gave him whatever he wanted from the bellies of the girls and handsome fees besides. And soon Couviard had two assistants and a pretty dappled mare that pulled a smart yellow gig with red wheel rims.

Meanwhile the Sabots had long since married off all their hungry girls but one. She was harelipped and blind in an eye—ugly beyond the redemption of any dowry Sabot was prepared to offer. The Sabots put the farm in her name and entrusted the deed to Couviard. They also gave the girl several sacks of seeds and two hundred plows. They themselves went far away, some said to Algeria, with a nice bundle of gold coins in a money belt.

The girl had her babies without assistance, then died. Her young had no idea how to use the plows, or what to do with the seed, which they ate, along with the thatch of the roof and the furniture. Then, as in Mathilde's time, they began eating soil.

These girls were wild and furtive, larger than any hungry girls before, and hungrier. They even ate the bodies of the dead, it was said, beginning with their own mother, whose body was gone when Father Sempier, tipped by a neighbor, came to sprinkle it with holy water. No one would marry a girl from Sabot's place now, so the young men all swore. Yet now and then a youth disappeared.

One day Father Sempier—now an old man—was out hunting for mushrooms in the forest between Houviers and Lamouset. He heard a noise, a snuffling and grunting like a pig nosing for truffles.

"*Mère de Dieu!* In this forest!" he exclaimed, his mouth watering. But the fuss was only one of the missing boys, stuffing dirt in his mouth, writhing and shaking like one possessed. Beside him on the ground there poked from a bag a pewter candelabrum and an embroidered cloth.

When the boy saw the priest he bolted to the Sabot farm, where the discreetly trailing priest saw a number of huge, round, naked girls sitting like houses on the ground, their feet sticking out at the ends of thin little legs. The priest watched, astonished, as the young man disappeared inside a fat body.

Watching longer, the priest saw that each of the girls sitting on the ground had at least one young man living inside her. He saw the young men lean ladders against the hungry girls' sides so they could climb up on their shoulders and comb their hair and whisper in their ears. And he saw the hungry girls themselves dig up basketsful of dirt with their hands and eat them. One fellow drove a stage coach right into a girl's body, six horses and a sizeable carriage with a great deal of baggage on top and behind! Father Sempier thought of trying to reason with the girls, or at least with their swains, but his outrage, revulsion, pity, and shame warred so fiercely within him he could only sputter.

Later he spoke to his bishop, who considered calling in an exorcist but decided on a more politic approach. He dropped a word in the ear of Dr. Nevers, and soon enough the gendarmes began shoving the hungry girls onto big flat wagons and carting them off to the lunatic asylum at Anse-le-Marteau, the jail having too few accommodations.

In the asylum was a common room, a stone hall with high vaulted ceilings and thick, wide, heavy oak doors. With ropes and pulleys, the girls were pushed and pulled into the room, then left to be questioned later. It had taken all of one day, that night, and most of the next day and night to bring them in, for the largest had to be slid along inclined planes. Moreover the numbers of girls grew as word spread of the arrest. For suddenly families and neighbors realized how very tired they were of the girls. Even husbands were tired. It was one thing to visit the girls in their wallows and quite another to have them rooting around day in, day out. How convenient if they were lunatics, to be chained to their beds and forgotten!

The asylum was run by the Sisters of Sainte Marie Couverte; many of them were the daughters of the best families of the region. These sisters showed their usual kindnesses to those placed in their care. The food they doled out was what they ate themselves, watery porridge, blackened radishes, and shrivelled apples, all in modest portions. The girls ate what they were given and banged on their metal plates for more. Failing to get it—there was no more—they threw their plates at the stone walls with such force they made holes as big as cannon balls. Ah, the huge, sullen girls, who had glowered and mooed as they were herded into the asylum—they were now frenzied. They threw themselves at the doors, but the doors did not even shake. The girls then tugged at the bars on the windows, and some of the bars gave way, but the windows themselves were too small for the girls to climb through; they could only stare at the neatly plowed fields beyond the asylum walls.

"It was frightful to see their gloom," said the Mother Superior later.

Soon the girls were quarrelling over the possessions the guilty in-laws had sent with the married ones—toothbrushes, wash rags, embroidered linen towels, scented soap, rosaries, and even—though the wife in question could not read—a novel in a lavender wrapper. The most damaging altercation broke out over a wicker suitcase, nicely lined, with ribbons and covered boards to hold the clothes in place. In the suitcase was a change of underwear and a muslin nightgown made from curtains. All the hungry girls wanted the gown, and the mouselike felt slippers that went with it, some to wear but most to eat. The girls began clawing and pummeling each other, sitting on each other's chests to stop each other's breath. They twisted noses, snapped fingers, gouged eyes, kicked and bit and punched till every girl was a quivering hulk. The groans were heard all along the new road, as far away as Rouen and farther. Indeed, as far as Calais! Fishing boats at sea heard the girls, and rich people floating on their yachts. It has even been claimed that across the Channel the Archbishop of Canterbury heard!

The sisters sent for Father Sempier, who sent for Couviard, who sent for Bostiac. The now white-haired pharmacist proclaimed there was not enough morphine in all of France to stop the moaning, so the sisters did not demur when arthritic old Couviard painfully raised his pistol to the foreheads of the girls, one by one, though not before babies had crawled from holes in the stomachs of a few.

"These creatures are hardly human," said the sisters, crossing themselves repeatedly. "Holy Mother, hear our prayers. . . ."

Dr. Couviard said nothing. He was wincing as he put down the babies crawling from their *mamans*. The certificates of death—which no one challenged—were to say the girls and their infants had died of natural causes.

Father Sempier presided over their burial in an abandoned quarry a few miles from Houviers. They were covered with gravel, then with rubble, with mortar and bricks, and only then with earth. On top of the hill where the quarry had been, a fine stone chapel was erected, financed by auctioning the loot from the girls' bodies and selling the Sabot farm.

Several people of Houviers now make a nice living peddling relics of the girls at little booths near the chapel, though needless to say the chapel is consecrated to the Holy Mother. The most popular relics are splinters of bone said to have been blown from the bullet holes in the girls' heads. There are also small vials of dirt in which the concessionaires claim are *poux de terre*—dead ones, of course. And there are special little cakes, baked as puffs with nuts inside, called *poucettes*.

The tour guides who meet the busses laugh at the rumor that babies were born from some of the dead girls' bellies long after they were buried. The guides find equally amusing the rumor that these hardy infants dug and ate their way up out of the quarry and began luring men to bring food and wealth to out-of-the-way places.

"Food runs out, wherever one is," they say. "Money is spent and men disappear, along with teapots and platters. Can one really blame the hungry girls who are many feet beneath the grass?"

SNAKESKINS

In the Parsee city of Galub, there streak and glide in the ditches snaky creatures known as DJITSIS, which twine in the legs of camels and donkeys, and in the wheels of hand-carts, and slither up the peoples' robes. The young of this serpent are hatched from a mother's mouth like so many words, to shed her quick upon entering the world, a habit they continue in shedding their own skins, at every turn, streaking out of their past lives faster than you can pull your foot from your stocking.

This is the snake the mothers warn their daughters of; for it crawls up their pantaloons lithe and quick, penetrates to the veiled privates, insinuates itself into the purse between the legs to count the coin—mind you, just to count the coin. Then it slithers through the ravine in the buttocks' fastness to reconnoiter the ridge of the spine, taking a turn around the ears beneath the tent that hides the women's faces before nipping back down and out the pantaloons faster than a frog snaps a fly, and all in the innocent, insolent manner of a sauntering privateer's man on shore leave. And it is not just the privacy of the ladies' persons the djitsis invade. For the rammish men it is worse than being taken like a ewe of which the hind legs have been discomfortably stuff't in some horny conscript's boots. It is a violating species of invasion, as your invasions go.

Now once a comfortable Galubi merchant, Salah Dey Oum, a dealer in carpets, reclined on his cushions in his private rooms, having been served a beef and pomegranate stew at the soft, fair hands of Fatima, his wife. Digging between his teeth with an ivory pick to skewer some pomegranate seeds, he found he had impaled some djitsi skins. And though he jettisoned the skins at once, he could not shake off the specter of his violated mouth, which writhed in his dream like a butcher-shop liver fresh before his face. He spat to his right and then to his left and turned to spit behind himself, muttering curses. He called for a looking glass that he might examine his tongue and his gums. And he looked and spat and looked and spat, not once, but many times. Weeks, nay months, later, he was still spitting and muttering and staring at the image of his tongue in the looking glass. And seeing him so afflicted with peculiar habits and debilitating fears, his customers lost their confidence in his judgment and began to take their trade elsewhere. The servants whispered that he refused to take off his shoes at night for fear djitsis would curl where his feet had been. Everyone saw how he cowered before the rolled carpets stacked in his shop, and his helpers tittered behind their hands.

Yet even as his 'prentices jeered him, Fatima stood with her hands modestly clasped, betraying no hint of contempt or reproach. Now when Salah had given away all the household furnishings, railing and pointing at their djitsi-bearing crevices, he shuddered at the folds of his wife's clothing, three times gingerly tapped her shoulder, and shoved her out the door.

Fatima's parents had long since died. Though she had brothers, they would not have her, nor would her brothers-in-law. All her married children advised her she was too old to dower for a second marriage. They enjoined her return to her husband; meekly she shuffled back to his shuttered house, putting one foot before the other.

No one answered her knock on the door, though she waited a long time. Finally the servants of the neighbors poked their heads over the wall to whisper that Salah had left the place, wandered away, no one knew where. The house was about to be taken by someone else, who had already brought in some movables. . . .

Once again, Fatima put one foot in front of the other, not daring to raise her eyes. And she came soon enough to a quarter of the city where she was unknown. She was tired by then, and sat down, and held out her hand, palm up. Thus she became a beggar, sleeping in doorways and gutters. She who had been a modest, closeted wife, whose plump, cossetted body had nestled in cushions and silks, now ground her bones on paving stones and cradled her head against hitching posts. Even among the beggars her life was accounted hard, for she had no bowl for coins and was too timid to jostle the passers-by.

Yet though she had neither cloak nor blanket, the night wind's soughing did not alarm her. She was warmed by the djitsis streaking in and out of her clothing, covering her person with cast-off skins. For though the DJITSIS do discomfit and discountenance all other persons whose parts they explore, the docile Fatima they succoured and consoled. 'Tis said the paths the serpents travelled did clean and brighten behind them; washing her sooty person, they did heal her mendicant's sores and chase away her fleas and lice, so that over her ribs her chastened flesh was soon as fresh as a child's, her fragrance a maiden's. Snakeskins wreathed her brow as if to celebrate her cast-off miserable condition. And her life was wondrous long.

When one morning she did not wake up, though the sun burned bright on her wrinkled eyelids, the beggars who moved in to strip her of her rags noticed all her clothes were djitsi skins, woven of countless patches that crumbled to the touch. But for the bottoms of her feet, crusted and yellow, her corpse was ablush and silken. And the beggars bowed their heads before her sleek and lustrous hair and washed her body themselves, having gone without bread to buy the lemon-scented water. They carried her on their shoulders to the tower where the carrion birds come to pillage the bones of the dead. Yet the birds would not drive their beaks into her flesh, but only hovered above her, their handlike wingtips spread, their coarse squawking refined to a song as melodious and mournful as the dirge of high-paid mourners.

And a rich man carved above the door a motto which read, "Life a service, death a prayer." And the Galubis sealed the tower door and boarded up the windows. And for all I know she is up there still, the fair, fair bride of an unknown groom.

Thus began the cult of Fatima's Redemption, a sect whose most faithful members make their beds in the street near the shrine. They claim the divinest love of the Lord is in His messengers, the djitsis, that saw a woman more naked than any paramour, and flinched not nor faltered at flaws or age or disease, but healed what was wounded, cured what was ill.

Putting aside their clothes, the faithful lie very still to attract the snakes, gritting their teeth as the djitsis wriggle blithe in their chinks. Some men send their wives to wait salvation for them, plotting substitution when the djitsis commence the "Rapturous Gleaming."

At the Gleaming, 'tis claimed, djitsis will dive down through the open pores of the faithful to swim the inner seas of each body, perusing and blessing what it has been given no living person to fathom, his own organs, floating jellyfish. And in their circumnavigation, the djitsis will discover the seat of the soul, whether it be near the Heart or the Mind. Their kiss will bless its naked neediness; then, like a sailor shucking his pants in a brothel, Man will shed generations of death. And the sun will shine a gleaming path across the salt lagoon of his body, and he will travel it to glory, Forever.

Yet never since the redemption of Fatima's bread-begging flesh has the love of the snakes again cheated Death's messengers. Patient Fatima sleeps, breathless, in the tower, her memory taunting the seekers from whose fathers' fathers she begged. And the birds circle the tower, singing and spreading their handlike wings. Sometimes they swoop to eat the skins the djitsis shed in the street.

MILADY'S PLOY

In her *Annals of the Plum Blossom Court*, Lady Nakitan speaks of the fashion for game parks among the Kyonese noblemen of the twelfth century. In these parks were ponds in which hunters could admire the reflected trappings of their servants, horses and falcons. Lady Nakitan recalls Lord Kito, who leaned so far forward to admire the rippling image of his warrior's topknot, he fell headfirst into a pond in the emperor's game park near the Village of Denzu. His head stuck in the mud, he drowned. For many years Kito's legs poked from the pond, first flesh, then bones, creaking in the winds that dappled the water, mocking, said Nakitan, the death of the poet Li-Po, who drowned from a boat when he leaned to embrace the reflected moon.

Among those failing to heed Kito's warning were the Emperor Hamitai's stags, elegant specimens the gamekeeper had appropriated from other parks the length and breadth of the island of Kyono. So vain were these stags, Lady Nakitan relates, they stopped by the pond when the full moon cast a clear light and dallied without feeding to contemplate the shining orb trapped in their branching antlers.

During the years between Lady Nakitan's childhood and her maturity—it would be impolite to speculate on the exact number of years—there grew up a generation of stags that refused to knock off its antlers each autumn, as the stags had always done. They would not even rub them on bark to scrape off the moss which stained them green, like the tea served at court. And the antlers of these stags branched taller and fuller as the seasons passed, though the weight toppled the stags when they bent their necks to browse.

In winter many stags sank beneath their antlers' snowy weight, and flakes drifted over them. It became fashionable, one winter, to feed the fallen stags. Bulky in quilted kimonos, each wearing three pairs of socks, the ladies of the court picked their way through the snow, followed by servants with bales of hay on their backs. Even the empress, Kataka, tucked her hands into her capacious sleeves and shuffled through the snow.

The emperor and his courtiers watched the ladies from a lacquered pavilion-of-regard especially constructed near the pond. All smiled benignly as the ladies bent their knees to brush the snow from the heads of prostrate stags, tendering bunches of hay from the tips of long red fingernails. The most beautiful lady, all observers agreed, was Kataka, the only one who did not interrupt the pageant to blow on her freezing fingers. By imperial decree, she alone was permitted to carry the small red dogs, the totojoni, in her sleeves. When her hands became cold, she simply warmed them in the breath of the dogs.

Kataka's discretion and grace so enchanted Hamitai he foreswore his concubines on the spot, but his resolution soon failed him. He began yielding to their blandishments once again, spending very few nights in his wife's bed, for still she failed to bear him the legitimate son he yearned for. The emperor considered taking a new wife, but Kataka lost no opportunity to divert his attention to the chase, so he did not bother to put her aside.

Yet in the matter of hunting, the imperial will was also thwarted, for the stags with the tree-tall antlers were dying faster than the emperor and his lords could hunt them. Moreover, they were failing to mate with the does, for if they reared to mount, their heavy antlers toppled them. Some of the does tried to slink beneath the standing stags, so they might be penetrated without having been mounted, but their stalky legs splayed out shaking beneath them. Then the emperor brought strong warriors from the coastal fortifications that the Kyonese guarded against the barbarous Man-Tsu. He charged these warriors swing their swords against the antlers of the chaste stags; alas, those who had lost their crowns hid in the trees and starved.

Hamitai wept at the prospect of losing the glorious stags forever. The ladies of the court consoled him with songs and dances, kites and puppets, flowers and tea, yet still he sunk into lethargy, voicing gloomy thoughts about an heir.

Unbeknownst to him, the Lady Kataka had been sneaking out of her room late at night, dressed in boy's clothing. She went to the kennel, for she had been training her dogs to perform certain tricks. Oh, several of the dogs could already walk on their hind legs, or roll over upon command, or speak or play dead. The training for these ordinary tricks Kataka left to the kennel's keepers, snoring in their huts the nights the lady whispered in the ears of her favorite dogs.

Because the sleeves of her boy's clothing were narrow, the empress

trained the dogs to follow each other behind her. And a wakeful Lady Nakitan, restless in the Plum Blossom Courtyard, watched in amazement as
a slender boy with a courtesan's undressed hair cascading down his back
strode purposefully into the game park, followed by an orderly file of small
red dogs, their plumy tails curled above their backs.

Concealed behind a pillar, Nakitan watched several nights; even in rain,
the boy's delicate head protected by a brilliant waxed paper umbrella, the
odd little column set forth in the night, returning only as the morning sun
began its rise.

One day Nakitan watched Kataka nodding on the throne as her kennel
keepers put the totojoni through their paces before the court, leading the
game little dogs to turn sommersaults in air, retrieve tossed arrows while
leaping through fiery hoops, form a shaky living pyramid on the back of a
trotting war horse. Lady Kataka yawned into her sleeve through the whole
performance, stroking her eyelids when the dogs danced in a rain of chry-
santhemum petals.

That very day Lady Nakitan bade her own servant go disguised to purchase a suit of boy's clothing. Dressed in the pants and simple coat, Nakitan watched in the Plum Blossom Courtyard, waiting to see her counterpart
walk through the moon-dappled night trailing dogs. And when the cortege
passed, Nakitan followed into the park.

There she saw Kataka feeding the deer dried currants, spindled on her
nails like beads on the wires of an abacus. In this way the empress had gained
the trust of the deer, and they clustered around her with the totojoni.

When Kataka pointed a currant-beaded finger, a totojon bitch backed
beneath a stag and tickled its member by wagging her tail—a coarse trick
Lady Nakitan felt a deep shame in watching, let alone recording. Yet so com-
pelling was her curiosity, so intense her desire to faithfully recount all the
singular events of her era, she did not fail to watch successive evenings as
Lady Kataka, through a series of vulgar tricks—over most of which Lady
Nakitan has been gracious enough to draw the veil of her discretion—proceeded to train the totojoni to mate with the deer in the following manner:
A totojon dog—the dogs are slightly larger than the bitches—stands beneath
the belly of a stag. This dog has on his back a bitch. She lowers herself on her
front paws, presenting her rump to the stag's member, having curved her tail
between her legs to cover the actual entrance to her body. The stag, teetering
beneath his burden of antlers, careful not to lose his balance, spills his seed

on her tail.

The bitch leaps from the back of the dog and rubs herself against the stag's knee-backs to pick up his scent. She then leaps once again onto the back of the dog this time backwards, her head toward the dog's tail. The dog runs up behind a doe; the backward bitch on the dog's back swives the doe with her delicate tail.

Seated alone in the pavilion-of-regard one fine spring day, the gloomy Hamitai was startled by the unexpected appearance of the totojoni, each wearing a brocade tabard, fanning out among the deer. At a word from their mistress, superbly arrayed in a robe embroidered with blue plum blossoms, the dogs proceeded to perform the trick that was henceforth known as the sleeve-dog ploy.

When most of the does bore young that summer, Hamitai dismissed all his concubines, sending them into a nunnery to contemplate the cycle of changing seasons. He himself vowed to live faithfully with his remarkable empress, who gave birth to three sons in the years that followed. The Dojan dynasty thus prevailed for another four centuries, though the emperors repeatedly called the warriors from the coastal fortifications to hunt the great-antlered deer.

To dignify the contest—for the stags could not run from the hunters and the fleet-footed does the hunters came to think it unmanly to kill—the hunters dressed in suits of armor so heavy and confining they had to be moved from place to place by attendants. They wore blindfolds over their eyes and shot at the stags heavy jeweled arrows that wavered on course. A man might have spent a lifetime firing these arrows before he hit a stag. With the warriors so preoccupied, the Man-Tsu, invading from the sea in 1637, found Kyono easy to conquer.

Fierce but intelligent, the conquerors decided against sacking the imperial palace, which they merely appropriated, dispatching the last Dojan emperor and his hunt-besotted courtiers to exile far in the interior of Man-Tsu country. The emperor's wife and concubines were permitted to remain in service. The conquerors, whose own women strode like men in flat shoes, considered the totojoni effete. The most succulent young pups they killed and ate; the rest they released into the game park, where the little dogs learned to hunt for food.

By night packs of feral totojoni harried the flanks of exhausted stags and pregnant does. When these collapsed, the totojoni ate them. By day, they ran with the deer, their tongues lolling between smiling black gums, performing the sleeve-dog ploy to sustain the future of their prey.

Time passed, and the fingernails of the Man-Tsu ladies grew longer. The Man-Tsu lords, forgetting they had once slept in their saddles, relacquered the pavilion-of-regard and sipped green tea, watching the dogs and the deer. Their sorcerors claimed the sight revived jaded potency, particularly in old men.

As the Man-Tsu relaxed their vigilance, the grandsons of the Dojan lords came out of the Man-Tsu homelands where their fathers and grandfathers, though married to Man-Tsu women, had secretly passed on the Dojan precepts of virtue, wisdom and pride. The grandsons took up arms in the name of the Kyonese people, many of whom now considered themselves Man-Tsu and cleaved to their conquerors.

The length and breadth of the island of Kyono became a battlefield; not a village escaped the battle, which lasted thirty-three years. Then a strong man, Nizan the Calm, rose from among the Dojan partisans and massacred the Man-Tsu, avenging his ancestors.

Lady Nakitan had long since died. It is to later chroniclers we must turn to piece together accounts of the legendary Nizan's life. There follows a story connecting the hero to the deer and the dogs of the game park, a story composed by Nanso, the singer of the Inn of the Unknown Blossom at Denzu.

Nizan the Calm had a sword-belt toggle of antler ivory carved in the shape of a sleeve dog's head. In the last days of the struggle for the Village of Denzu, which had nestled all along by the wall that surrounded the emperor's park, Nizan appeared in Denzu, by then a village mostly of widows, dressed as a seller of charcoal, in a plain blue smock, a bandanna tied around his head, his sword hidden in the bundle he carried on his back. Whispering through the bamboo wall of the garden of the Unknown Blossom, Nizan spread rumors that one of the Man-Tsu protector's men considered another a coward. The second thought the first was ugly, while both thought a third was bestial and stupid. Over such trifles, all the protector's men fought to death among themselves, all but the lord protector himself, Hosai, whom the widows saw creeping from his compound, hiding in the shadow of each house he passed, the luster of his armor dimmed by dust. He had last been seen as an eddy of dust on the road.

Nizan unbundled his sword and stripped off his smock. He drank rice wine at the Inn of the Unknown Blossom. One widow sang to entertain him; another combed his long hair and refashioned his topknot. Others brought him robes of embroidered silk and washed and perfumed his feet.

As word spread of Nizan's calm deportment, many Man-Tsu sympathizers came to capitulate, sitting on the mats around him. Some were scarred veterans in battered armor, others plump pleasure-seekers.

"Master," said all, "we have heard of your virtue, have come to serve you, hoping to bear ourselves well in the reign of peace. To prove our sincerity, we offer you coins, scrolls and embroideries. We touch our foreheads to the floor."

One supplicant, Bardo, was a laughable rustic with a bright red nose. He wore a coarse linen blouse, a straw hat and leggings.

"Master," he said, "my parents are dead. I have left my wife to harvest the rice and keep what she can in the mouths of seven children. Yet I too have come to pay homage to Virtue and Wisdom. I will sit in the back, not touching these illustrious ones. I offer my rice-straw shoes."

Nizan permitted all supplicants to sleep on the floor, to eat from ordinary bowls, even the most refined of them. Daily Nizan sat in their midst, saying nothing.

One afternoon the Calm One was gazing at a scroll, painted by the prettiest widow, showing a clump of grass blades flattened before a storm. The characters read "Strength is not revealed without occasion." Nizan sipped his wine. He polished on his sleeve a plum the cleverest widow had handed him. He picked his teeth with a silver pick from the oldest widow, although his teeth were clean; he had eaten nothing but a soup of lotus root. He toyed with his sword-belt toggle of antler ivory carved in the shape of a sleeve dog's head. Still he said nothing.

Bardo crawled forward, touching his forehead to the floor three times. He plucked at the hem of Nizan's robe. "Master," he said, "how can you be the harbinger of righteous peace if your talisman is carved of the craven stag's antler in the shape of the pandering dog?"

Nizan looked out the window. The square was empty now where after the battle the children of the poorest widows had looted the bodies of the dead. Their mothers had watched silent in doorways. The dead, stripped of their clothing, had gleamed in the moonlight. The moon herself had peeped from the clouds above the game park as the youngest widow now peeked from behind a screen, lowering her head to show Nizan the nape of her neck.

Bardo grew restless waiting for an answer and asked his question again, plucking at Nizan's sleeve. The skin of the plum the Calm One was polishing glistened like glazed blood. He glanced at the upturned faces around him, as if soliciting a reply. Then, pulling from its scabbard his lacquer-handled sword, Nizan chopped off his own topknot.

"Master!" gasped the supplicants.

Nizan bit into the plum. Shrugging, he knocked off Bardo's red putty nose, thus dislodging the rustic's hat to reveal a topknot dressed in the Man-Tsu style. Bardo forthwith disembowelled himself with Nizan's politely offered sword, which the Calm One wiped on the dying man's leggings, calling out for more plums. The children of the poorest widows began stripping the body of Lord Hosai. And still the supplicants were silent.

"Ah!" sighed Nizan, bowing his head. "Soon we will sit in the pavilion-of-regard, as our ancestors did." Looking down at Hosai, he answered Bardo's question, pitching his words one by one like small white stones into a dark, still pond: "I had only to look at my own heart's wish to prevail."

THE CHANGE

Through telescopes we see them still, the doggy mutants, trotting over Hanewok Island in the Tongtu Atoll's debris, scanning air and dust with thin red snouts, then shivering, jolted. Their green fur ruffs stand on end; bright blue feather crests vibrate. They poke their snouts at the jolts and drink.

We have registered the jolts on our counters since 1953, when a cloud bloomed over the Tongtus, miles of Pacific were showered with poison and ash, and the waters reared to swamp the islands, claiming all but Hanewok. The creatures that had lived there, a species of rat, a species of pig—ran to the sea to cool the cooking meat they had become; the surface of the sea was littered with fish. Nor did the birds escape, returning to the island to nest as the ashes cooled. Their eggs had thin shells, though the young inside were too weak to peck out. It was just as well. Their parents were too weak to feed them, or feed themselves, which was just as well, for there was nothing to eat. Death and more death. The jungle had rotted beneath the ash; windborne seeds neither thrived nor rooted. Only the neones—never there before—the neones thrived.

The bitches often chase each other, rolling on their backs and waving their paws. They perk pointed ears half-hidden in their ruffs; their eyes' facets wink in the glare of the sun. They bark at their shadows and stalk the waggly snakes of their tails.

Beneath the tails sway the buds of flowers, fuschia and orange and red. Sometimes the flowers open. Their stamens darken from ocher to red-brown. The petals fall, and orange fruit ripens on the flowers' sepals.

Seeing the bitches swing fruit between their legs, observers at first thought them male. Then Dr. William Smith, a biophysicist employed by the U.S. Army, watched the fruit burst in the tunnel of his view, seeds puff out in a mushroom cloud. His sequenced photographs show bitches with stiffened tails plowing furrows to plant the seed, young sprouting snout-first in litters that look like patches of grass. Gradually eyes and crests appear, then ruffs. When front paws emerge, the young dig out their hind parts. Already their eyes swivel, their snouts track.

The bitches seem to have no natural enemies. Smith in his early years of watching saw only the aged die, their ruffs and snouts fading before them.

When a neone dies, the surviving bitches gather around her body. The small mouths beneath their snouts open as if they were keening. They dig a hole in the ash with their forepaws, nudge the body into it with kicks of their hind legs, and scuff ash on it. They hunt no jolts until the sun has risen and set three times.

After viewing from Nahman Island his first neone "memorial service," as Smith persisted in calling it, he, a solitary bachelor who had only cared for his work, could not bear to look in his telescope for days. He was no longer hungry for the food he spooned from cans and cooked on a hot-plate. He could find no repose on his cot by the telescope. Again and again, he circumambulated the tiny observatory island, crowding its beaches with footprints.

In his official reports, Smith began calling the bitches by name, as if he could tell them apart at so great a distance. His superior officer, Colonel Laurence Fuller, detailed a clerk to count the names mentioned in one report. The clerk lost count at 110. "Crook-Tail," "Long-Shank," "Flop-Ear," "Tail-Dragger," "Leap-Lady," and "Sprinter" were most frequently mentioned.

"Naming absurd," Fuller radioed Smith. "Naming bacteria seen in a microscope. Desist."

There was no reply from Smith. Several days later, he ordered through the mail a flute, and after it had arrived he sat on the concrete stoop of his Quonset hut playing strange melodies of his own devising. He said neither hello nor good-bye to the soldiers who had come by helicopter to deliver his supplies. For the duration of his tour of duty, he spoke to no one except to radio that supplies were needed, reports ready.

The reports continued to be more voluminous than Fuller liked, and couched in unscientific language.

"He thinks he's writing a novel," Fuller confided to a colleague.

But the post was such a desolate one, the work itself, involving hours at the telescope, so dreary, Fuller despaired of finding another scientist suited for it. He did not recall Smith even when he was insubordinate, refusing to take the leaves he was ordered to take "for the sake of his emotional balance." Fuller merely sighed and continued to have each report summarized and rewritten as it came in, though he attached Smith's originals to his staff's translations before sending them on.

Some of Fuller's superiors had questions, not, it turns out, about the reports, but about the supplies Smith ordered—the seeds, for instance, and the turkeys and goats.

"Does he think we're running an agricultural station?"

"Give the man what he wants," Fuller wearily insisted.

Though Fuller feared a flap or an investigation, there was none, not even when Smith balked at "the Army way," as when he asked that future deliveries of supplies to Nahman be made by non-motorized craft. The noises of motors and engines, he said, were overpopulating Hanewok.

Bitches frightened, as of aircraft noise, dig shallow gravelike burrows for themselves, wrote Smith in a report. They heap mounds of ashes on their own heads, leaving their tails and flowers exposed. The flowers open. Clouds of specks emerge from the animal's ruffs to fly into their flowers. These specks are males, Smith explained. Only during a scare do they swarm from the ruffs; only then do the flowers open, the stamens turn red-brown.

After a U.S. Air Force maneuver in June, 1976, so many neones were born that bitches were crowded into the sea. The levels of radiation detected on the island dropped dramatically. Smith reported seagulls successfully rearing young on Hanewok, grass springing up, and sapling palms putting forth fronds.

Neones grew fewer, and these had desperate ribs, scraggly ruffs and crests. When frightened they buried their heads as before, but the speck clouds were wispier; many stamens did not darken.

In late 1976 young bitches began to drop in their tracks while playing. The survivors gathered to mourn as before. Sometimes they had to be buried themselves.

Soon there will be no neones, Smith predicted. The island will blossom a tropical paradise, the bones of neones be uncovered by hotel builders.

"Don't you see you are killing the hope of the world?" he wrote to Fuller.

Fuller suppressed the strange communication. However, he approved Smith's request for copies of all available literature, published and unpublished, on the macro- and micro-effects of the bombings of Hiroshima and Nagasaki; on the radioactive wastes of nuclear-energy plants; on the underground and desert bomb tests of various nations. . . .

Shortly after there began a series of letters between Smith and Fuller, Smith now addressing his superior in more appropriately crisp language than before, and Fuller often replying in longhand rather than dictating to a clerk-typist.

Smith first proposed that teams of trappers be sent to Hanewok dressed in shield-suits against residual radiation. They were to net neones for transport in lead-lined ships and trucks to the mainland salt mines where atomic power-plant wastes are stored. The barrels containing the radioactive wastes would be tapped and neones turned loose to forage.

"This practice," Smith claimed, "would not only save neones from extinction but allow humans to benefit from nuclear energy without exposure to the peril of its wastes."

Fuller reminded Smith of an earlier supposition (long since discarded, Smith would insist) that neones might need sunlight to live, that part of their food might be made in their ruffs from light. Since salt mines are dark, reasoned Fuller, neones would wither surrounded by food. Meanwhile, the trappers would have been pointlessly exposed to radiation.

Smith proposed that electricians in shield-suits be sent to the salt mines to rig powerful light sources duplicating the spectrum of rays emitted by the sun.

Fuller pointed out that the electricians should not be asked to risk death for the neones' sake.

"Whatever the level of radiation on Hanewok, the level at the waste-dump sites is high."

"If one electrician in a shield-suit would enter those mines, they need never cast death-spells again," said Smith.

Fuller pointed out that no such upshot was certain.

"We cannot say we know that neones metabolize radioactivity. Only laboratory study," insisted Fuller, "will establish a consensus on their true nature."

Fuller proposed that a shield-suited Smith proceed in a quiet craft to Hanewok to bring back a neone for laboratory study. Smith readily agreed, but Fuller only replied that Smith had failed to detect the irony of the proposal. No agency, he said, would fund a laboratory to safely house the bitch, who might, he said, be radioactive herself, would certainly require radioactive food, and might carry radioactive "mates" in her ruff.

Smith noted the counters' proof that radiation on Hanewok had dropped to a level humans can sustain even without shield-suits—a level equivalent to a chest X-ray's. He suggested that the island be test-dusted with seeds, that test pairs of animals, rats and goats, cats and monkeys and frogs, be parachuted in.

"If these survive," said Smith, "can man not approach the garden?"

Fuller noted that the genetic consequences for test animals could not be documented for years, if at all. Moreover, the residual radioactivity that had generated at its peak the mutant neones might still generate other species. New diseases might foam over the world, born of parasites carried by the test animals.

"What if the specks you call neone males are viruses?" asked Fuller. "Might they not infect other species?"

"Only those with flowers beneath their tails," quipped Smith.

Fuller said the subject under discussion should not elicit jokes.

What could one do but laugh? asked Smith. On Hanewok neones were dying in numbers he characterized as alarming.

Fuller asked whether Smith would like to be sent a dog, to keep him company and to help him maintain his objectivity.

Shortly after, Smith resigned his commission. He packed his bags and stowed his gear in his emergency raft. He is thought to have set out from Nahman for Hanewok with seeds, tubers, turkeys, goats, the King James version of the Bible, a silver flute, a portable X-ray machine, tools, a nylon tent, and spare parts for the X-ray machine's generator. He carried no shield-suit and no radio.

The post on Nahman Island has been effectively vacant since Smith's decampment. The last man assigned to it became deranged, believing at last that his radio had turned on him. Before he was removed from the island, he did say he had observed Smith lying in a hammock among the neones, but then Smith seems to have moved to the other side of Hanewok.

Smith's next-to-last official communique (before his evacuation to Hanewok) announced a discovery scholarly if not scientific.

"I have found it," he wrote, "in a book of diaries of the survivors of Hiroshima. There was a young man who had been so badly exposed to the rays he threw up black blood. He did not leave the area of the bomb blast, however, but moved further into it, advancing to within a view of the very crater. He would look on his death before succumbing to it, so he said.

"Perhaps if he had abandoned the bomb-blast site he would not have died, or he might have lived many more months or even years. Then again, perhaps if he had come closer to the neones they would have healed him. Yes, neones. Clearly he saw neones. Here are the words of Hirao Kumaki, a Japanese science student twenty-five years old in 1945:

"'At first I thought they were eating the blast, but now I think they are eating the sadness. And I would like to think they have always been here on earth. Wherever there has been an incredible destruction, there these dogs with the gay bright eyes and the little folded hands of insects, these dogs with bird crests, lion ruffs, and flowers beneath their tails, have trotted sniffing and sucking. I would like to think that. The creatures may be an illusion, a dream I am vouchsafed or indulge myself because I know I will soon die. Yet they ignore me. They are absorbed with themselves, in flashing their glittering eyes. Surely the flashing of the facets of their eyes is a signal—perhaps to mates. Just as the lights in the tails of fireflies say, "I am here, I am here," so do the eyes of the animals before me. Or perhaps they do not signal each other at all, but rather a god or a being from space, a being or beings more evolved than we humans; that is my hope. "I am here," say the creatures. "Here and listening. I am ready for what is to come. For the change."'"

AURAVIR

The yellow-haired monkeys known to the Romans as "golden men" are now extinct, though once they foraged the known world. Historian Veratius Aurelius spoke of watching a large band near Colchis, on the eastern shore of the Black Sea, grazing on leaves and fruit, grubbing for seeds and roots, and storing food for winter in hollow trees.

"Auravirs," said Veratius, "have thumbs and are dextrous. In winter they roll snow into head-high balls; in summer they weave cloaks and hats of grass. They pound berries into paste and dye the fur around their faces and genitals.

"In spring, the yearlings marry, their mothers arranging matches through exchanges of nutshells. The infants are born hairless and naked; they live at their mothers' breasts in tree nests, their fathers guarding the feet of the trees without closing their eyes even to sleep.

"Day and night the fathers watch, swinging as lanterns their gold-brown eyes. They comb their fur with their fingers, fluffing their jowls and tails and straightening the skirts at their haunches. They croon 'oola oola oola. . . . '"

Veratius observed auravirs chanting to the beat of log drums, tossing and leaping and stamping. He claimed to have danced with the auravirs, who dyed his pubic hair and eyelids blue.

Veratius quoted from the earlier writing, lost to us in its entirety, of the Greek chronicler Sophides, who claimed that Prometheus was an auravir. His name was Pelau-thelau in the auravir language. He was only a child when captured by human bandits. They cajoled him with bits of pomegranate to reveal the trick of fire, which auravir children had learned playing with sticks, then they bound him and left him to starve. His parents searched for him day and. night. They did not stop even to hunt for food. They called "Pelau-thelau! Ahoo, ahoo, ahoo," but their son did not answer, and when they found him he was dead. They offered his body to crows. After his flesh had been eaten, they pissed on his hide to cure it and hung it in their nest.

Sophides believed the so-called golden fleece was two golden fleeces, the hides not of rams but of auravirs. According to him, King Athamas of Thessaly was married to the auravir Nefu-waleah. Athamas, known as "The Gloomy," had taken no wife before, though his beard was grizzled and his hands were gnarled. Before Nefu-waleah, no female had attracted his attention. He often sat on his throne for hours, without moving or speaking, his head sunk into his chest. No dancer could arouse him, nor juggler amaze him. He often neglected to bathe, and his beard was hung with bits of food. The ladies of the court tittered behind the pillars of the hall; Athamas permitted their disrespect, and soon foreign ambassadors, even couriers, barely bowed in his presence. The name of Thessaly bore less and less weight in the councils of warriors, and Athamas's courtiers looked to turn the situation.

Seeing Nefu-waleah led into the marketplace, a rope around her neck, by some trappers, who hoped to sell her to be baited by dogs, the oldest among the courtiers purchased her to give to the king.

No sooner had she been presented than she began combing the king's beard with her fingers, chuckling beneath her breath. To the great amusement of the court, she inspected his head hair by hair for lice. She tickled his feet and fed him bits of fruit with her toes. Once or twice he raised his head and stared at her.

She could juggle sixteen plates and play hour-long trills on the harp. She could turn quadruple sommersaults and glide through the air from pillar to pillar. She would walk up to a peacock, singing "noo nah inah inooh" and bobbing her head. The peacock would permit her to stroke his neck, to dust his crest, and even to pluck his tail feathers. Flying birds came to Nefu-waleah, finches and wrens, larks and nightingales. Clinging to a pillar high above the court, she called them out of the air, "acri acri acri. . . ." They flew through the windows and sang for the king, "tooee tooee tooee. . . ."

The day Nefu-waleah showed herself to Athamas with eyelids and genitals dyed bright blue, he announced to the court that he would marry her. He changed her name to Nephele.

At her wedding banquet, Nephele would not eat the quail tongue the king would have fed her with his own hands, but she smacked her lips as she munched a cockroach that had been scuttling under his chair. After several bowls of wine, some of which she poured on her head, she perched on top of a statue of the king's father, peeled a pomegranate, and smeared its juice on her earlobes and nipples. She danced for the king her snake dance, standing perfectly still and moving only her tail. She sang for the king, "nunchi oola, nunchi oola, nunchi oola oola. . . ."

The citizens of Thessaly were pleased that the king had married. They celebrated the birth of a son, Phryxus, and a daughter, Helle, with days of eating and nights of dancing. But as it became clear that Phryxus would one day succeed his father on the throne, the citizens began to mutter. Athamas's courtiers—including the old man who had brought Nephele to the king—began to whisper about the prince. They asked the citizens whether they wished to be ruled by a king who ate flies and whose language was a rain of bird calls. How would a king who hung from the capitals of pillars judge disputes? With what honor to the kingdom could a king who scratched his ears with his feet receive visits from royal persons? How could a king who ate worms hope through marriage to promote a useful alliance?

Athamas at first resisted the importunities of his courtiers; he yielded at last to a delegation of citizens whose heads had been sprinkled with ashes. He renounced Nephele and her children and married a princess of Macedonia selected by his courtiers. Soon after, his beard was as dirty as ever; the new queen, who was only thirteen years old, announced to the court that she would not sit on the king's lap any more because he smelled.

With the help of servants whose palms Athamas had crossed with silver, Nephele and her children fled the palace ahead of the assassins the courtiers had hired. Golden-haired Nephele and her two golden children fled through the treetops, gliding from tree to tree; hence the legend that the golden "rams" flew through the air.

"Now whenever the moon is full," claimed Veratius, "the citizens of Thessaly hide beneath their beds so as not to hear the howls of grief and rage from the treetops. They say that Nephele and her children return to shake the branches of trees so hard the leaves fall off at the height of summer. Thessalians who venture from their houses are pelted with sticks, with feces, and even with stones. Squatting in the treetops Nephele and her children shake their fingers at the citizens and scold them. They sing 'toli kapapapa toli kapapapapapa' and laugh until the sun comes up."

Sophides believed Nephele crossed the Dardanelles hanging from the stern of a wine merchant's ship. Curled in Nephele's fur, Helle's fingers tired, and she fell into the sea at Hellespont. The ship's sailors discovered the mother and Phryxus because they were obstructing the movement of the rudder. The sailors brought them to the court of Aetes of Colchis—the next landfall—as a gift of slaves.

Because of his appetite for female flesh, Aetes was known as "Dove Impaler." In his youth he had been called "Father of Grass" because his children were as common as grass in the kingdom. In his elderly years, his interest in the long-legged Colchean maidens waned.

His tastes become exotic, he preferred to mount foreign women, especially slaves, and so his courtiers vied at auctions to purchase Nubians, Circassians, and Phoenicians. Some said the king's appetite for slaves was feigned, that his hunger was all for his daughter, Medea, despite her pock-marks and club foot; others said the love between father and daughter was of the tenderest sort. There were those who whispered that Medea had bewitched her father with a mixture of dried dragon testicle and pounded staghorn, an enchantment she had learned from foreign magicians, but where she had met these magicians none could say. There were no foreign magicians at court, and Medea never travelled.

Medea was Aetes' soothsayer. Daily she disembowelled a chicken to read its entrails. At a black look from her above the guts of a hen, the most bat-tle-scarred warriors in the kingdom quivered.

Except when the king retired to his bedroom to await a concubine, Medea was always at her father's side. Some said the king mounted women only to torture his daughter, who watched through a hole in the ceiling. Oth-ers said Medea chose her father's concubines and afterward changed them to fowl or to dogs.

Certainly the courtyard of the palace, and even the great hall, was thronged with dogs, for the king was fond of hunting. He had been known to set captive Amazon maidens loose in his woods and to hunt them with hound and spear. After the king had mounted their corpses, Medea turned them to boars. They were served with apples in their mouths at a great feast to which all the citizens of Colchis, and even the slaves, were invited. This was the generosity of Aetes.

The wife of the king was mad. She cowered in the shadows of the great hall playing peekaboo with his guards. They pitied her and often hid her from Medea, who made her mother crawl on all fours to food tossed on the ground. Some said Medea hated her mother for expelling her from the womb before her foot was fully formed. Others said Medea only bullied her mother to please the king and protect her mother from his crueler whims. They said Medea slept with her mother most nights, curled between her breasts. They said Medea only waited a chance to poison her father.

When Nephele and Phryxus were brought to the court, dressed in clean white tunics and garlanded with flowers, the king raised his eyebrows. Staring at Nephele's bandy yellow legs, he tapped the tips of his fingers together. He whispered in Medea's ear.

Nephele's wrists had been tied behind her back to prevent her pulling the fur from her chest in grief at the death of her daughter, the loss of her husband. Phryxus's hands had not been bound, and he amused the court with headstands and cartwheels, as if to distract the Colcheans.

Nephele gazed out the window at the sea as handmaidens led her to a wardrobe. She chattered and whimpered softly, but allowed herself to be dressed in a gauze gown. So docile was she that the servants unbound her hands before leading her to her place of honor in the torchlit procession to the king's bed.

Finger cymbals clinked. Horns whined. Dancing girls scattered rose petals as the procession began to move. Howling for Phryxus, "aa ooh aa ooh aa ooh," Nephele climbed to the top of a window, wrapped her tail around her throat and strangled herself.

Phryxus darted from the hall, seized Nephele's body from the ground where it lay broken, and escaped with it over the palace wall through the trees. None of the dogs would track him, although they were given a mantle to sniff that had fallen from Phryxus's shoulders.

Phryxus came at last to a sacred grove in which only priests were allowed to set foot. The guards chasing him tore their tunics and screamed "Sacrilege!" but Phryxus did not come out. Crows descended into the branches of the sacred trees; the guards cut their faces with their fingernails and rubbed ashes and dirt into the wounds. They sang "sae sae sae sae" and circled the grove holding laurel boughs. They sang "fa fa fa fa," shouting through the mouthpieces of mud masks and waving strips of goat's flesh above their heads. Phryxus did not emerge from the grove, and even the priests would not set foot in it while he remained, tainting the home of the god with corrupt flesh, inviting to eat at the god's own table the birds of death.

Sophides believed that Phryxus remained in the grove until Medea gave some wandering cutthroats—foreigners who did not fear the god—poisoned grain and the promise of the hides. The foreigners entered the grove naked but for feathers Medea had glued to their bodies with mud. They sang "tooee tooee tooee" and shook the poisoned grain in bowls.

Soon after Phryxus's death, the grove of the god withered and died. Plague and famine struck Colchis, and the citizens asked Medea and Aetes to disembowel themselves on the altar where Medea had read the future in the bodies of birds. The citizens hunted down the bandits, reclaimed the golden hides, and hung them in the withered grove, guarding them day and night. In time new shoots sprang from the dead wood of the sacred trees, but the trees never grew large and strong again. Yet it came to be said that nowhere in the world did the birds sing more sweetly than in the ruined grove near the empty palace in the poor country of Colchis.

Veratius noted that auravirs were becoming fewer; he guessed they were migrating eastward to escape bandits and slavers. Yet before the auravirs had vanished from history, the princely Persian chronicler Farshid Marsad had recorded his belief that certain winter apparitions troubling the dreams of shepherds in the valleys of the Elburz Mountains were remnant auravirs, their fur turned white in the snow that drifts against huts and rocks. The creatures hover beyond the light of the fire till the shepherds sleep, hoping to steal grains of rice stuck in the bottoms of their cooking pots.

SALT

You sit before me your heart a cup, and who am I to gainsay you drink? Not that I recall the days of living under the waves, before the slukie drove us into the fire of air. Yet I have heard of thousands of galiven laying each two eggs on the beach come spring. We had to fight the gulls for vollow room, though when we had mounded the walls, the gulls still dove to steal the eggs, so small and pearly. We could not leave the vollows to fish; we sat on our heels growing thinner. We watched the swooping gulls, and we watched the waxing moon, pulling the tide higher and higher. And when the moon was very full and very bright, and the tide rose very high, then the salt of Selukilim's seed was spilled in our nests, our eggs were quicked to life.

Soon enough the hatching babes would crawl about like worms. Their eyes were closed, but their noses open: *they* could find the mother milk. A woman's breasts then were slitties—two slits for the twin young that would cling to their mothers, licking till they heavied and dropped, the bony mothers could fatten again.

The women then were all great dreamers, weaving long lure-songs and singing them from sea to sky, though then there was no crack between us and the blue above; only a change, a shading of light, like hatching or death, and night the same. The moon was closer to us then; she had a face like ours and smiled. As we sang with our noses pointing up, fish and eels and oysters forgot the fear of our teeth. When our bellies were full, we'd comb our hair with fish bones, lining our vollows with shells so diving gulls would break their beaks.

In those days, many women withered to leather watching till their young had grown. Then Turrill One-Hand dreamed there were two mothers to each vollow, two wives. While one sang food, the other watched for gulls; together they waited for the tide to rise. And Turrill's dream became the song we lived. For every vollow two wives, four eggs. Many more young grew up than before, and fewer mothers starved. And it came to pass we lacked for vollow room.

Then was the lurking, the very first. A hungry wife turned her back on her vollow to spy her mate coming up with fish, the neighboring lurker cracked the eggs. No matter how the mother flailed her arms, or how she shrieked, the gulls dove. Sometimes the mother tried to hold the slithering egg stuff, keep it whole in the shells of her hands. Still it slipped between her fingers, yolk and white together (for in those days they were one) seeping the vollow chinks into sand. Sometimes the lurked mother covered the squirmy egg with her body, and she herself ate it.

Oh, we had not yet tears, so we did not weep, but lure-songs keened to woe-songs then, wails of grieving for our eggs. Still we weave the lurk-loss songs, feat nights that fall after laying, singing so we won't forget, though the woe palls the fish and eels. But I tell of a time long before, when broken eggs first soiled our chins.

In those gone days Va Long-Shank dreamed. She dreamed the vollows need not be by the sea. She dreamed the galiven could dwell further in, like the rabbits and mice. She dreamed we could eat the rabbits and mice. And she dreamed the vollow-mates could carry salt seed from the slukie's sea.

Stowing pinches of salt in the pockets of bone that held her eyes, Va hobbled on sleek and tender feet to the inland of her home isle. She made her vollow there, digging into a hill with Alin, her wife. They dug with their hands till their hands bled, then they dug with a stick till their fingers blistered. Finally they dug with a shovel, a shell lashed to a stick with vine. Oh, hearing the root-cut laundset say they first made shovels themselves, I don't see how they can tell such knownful lies! It was Va and Va alone; even her vollow-wife Alin would never have claimed that deed for own!

Other galiven followed Va, with salt in the pouches under their eyes. They chased the prey through the grasses crooning lure-songs. And the rabbits and mice stood front paws up with their ears turned, spelled as ever the fish and eels. Now the galiven lined their vollows with fur. They quicked their eggs with tides of tears, crying on each other's eggs, the one the other's slukie sea, so the young would wonder at strangeness all their lives, and their spells would be strong. Soon the inlands of our home isles were full as our shores.

Again it passed we lacked for vollow room; again we lurked our neighbors' eggs; again the lure-songs keened to woe, our prey fled the sorrow that palled the air so gray. Now our offspring were gloomy and listless, with foggy eyes and sullen tongues. Their songs were a long complaint, endless and stubborn as death; we wished they had never been born.

Then dreamed one of them, Hogil Long-Sight. Hogil dreamed we crossed the sea to a vastland over the edge of the world. No one but Hogil had seen this land. Where was it? All the sulky Hogil knew was far away. How could we get so far? We could swim in the sea to fish, but we did not like to swim beyond landsight.

When we had dwelt in the sea, long before, Selukilim, whose sea it was, ate our eggs as we dropped them, ate our young. She chased the women to bite off their limbs or even to gobble the small ones whole. Now whenever we looked out to sea, we saw Selukilim's eyes, head crest billowing spumy curls, nostrils snorting foam, tongue snake-quick. And sometimes the slukie rose in the shallows, picking her way across the rocks on webby hind feet. Then the women saw her scaly belly, wee front feet. They saw her whippy tail swishing and snapping. Sometimes her tongue-tip lolled between her teeth, giving her an oafish look. Yet when she roared from deep in her throat, the women crouched in their vollows, rounding their children in their arms, and no more peeped at the slukie so bold.

Hogil's mate, Pogeet Round-Nose, dreamed those who swam to the vastland were eaten by Selukilim, first their faces, then their limbs. What was left the fish ate. Pogeet woke screaming in darkness, feeling on her body the kiss of those fish. And Hogil suffered the dream of her mate as a stone in her ribs. She sat in a pall the whole next day and lay in the path of the moon that night. Though Pogeet laid fish before her, twitching fresh, with heads and tails bitten neatly off, Hogil left the gift-fish for gulls. She would not eat till a dream had haunted her wish-keen song.

"I see us riding the sea," she sang, "riding the sea as foam rides waves. We have made ourselves our own slukie by stretching the skins of fish over shovels and lashing the shovels with vines—the slukie's ribs. With other shovels we dig at the water and part it fast and strong as Selukilim herself. She fears us now; we ride an island that looks like her, and Oh, she fears herself."

And Hogil's dream became the song we lived. We made our slukie of singing and fish-skin, shovels and wishes, and did it in winter, when the wind blew snow in our faces.

Now we had been wont to roof our vollows with kelp and sleep through winter till our skin was pale as the bellies of fish, but the winter after Hogil's dream, we stayed awake. We held a song-feat to see who should ride in *Boldness*, the foam-riding slukie, named for the plaining, pushing strength of Hogil's dream. There were among us singers so strong they could hold a note from dawn to dusk to dawn again, neither gasping, nor quavering, nor blueing in the face. But Hogil was not among them. And when her voice gave out in the feat's first dusk, she rose in a pout. Yet she bowed her head and pledged herself down; and though her heart was sullen-sore, she told the brave what stars the dream had said to watch, what waters trust. When days and shadows lengthened, and eggs swelled in bellies, she joined her hands to ours to launch the strong-throats, for long was their way, and great their quest.

Then as we watched she walked out into the sea; a gull took her up in long-toed feet, flying with her out of sight. Sure she was gone. Pogeet her vollow-wife watched and faded and died, and her we shrouded and gave to the deep.

By the time the belly of *Boldness* scraped on the far-off shore, the sun had melted the riders' fat from their bones. Their skin was hard and dark, like the flesh of sun-dried fish. The slukie had followed them over the sea, worrying them too close to cast their spell for food. Yet had not the slukie's breathing driven *Boldness* fast ahead, the women might still be riding the waves, a crew of bones—that was the way it was.

And the so-called truest laundset say they invented bolds! And sails! And prows! And keels! And rudders! And rope! And oars! But those laundset were not yet. They have not *been* let alone forgot.

On the vastland shore the riders howled wild and shrill, naming themselves brave bolden. And stuffing their mouths with berries and fish, the bolden forgot their tears' hard birth, the stain of neighbor-lurking, the blot of vollow-warring. So while still a poke-belly fry, Magin Wide-Mouth dreamed she could cut and shape a reed to make a flute. First she blew a song of eggs and lengthening days, then a song of foam-tossed bolden spitting in the slukie's eyes. Yet as she blew she did not point her nose to the sky; her face was to Selukilim, witting not the slukie's force. And so poor Magin blew up the bane her mother's mother no longer knew: blew up vollow-warring, blew up neighbor-lurking. And song-pall darkened the sky and roiled the waves, and the eye-salt spilled. The grinking gulls clustered the air around Magin, as if her singing fed them, but we could not eat. For three days no woman spelled a fish or an eel.

"We are sinking back to Selukilim's sea," cried some. They twisted Magin's arms behind her back. They tromped her flute and shoved her away from the reeds. Whenever Magin opened her mouth, they covered it up with their hands. Then in the dark of a night when the others slept, so many song-motes rose in her throat she choked, biting with her long teeth through her own hands that covered her mouth.

The bolden wove a shroud of reeds; weighting Magin down with stones, they dropped her to the fathomy deep.

"Go bubble your fearsome wishes underwater," they said. Yet salty old woe, the seed of home, was in their eyes. How could they leave it behind?

Soon after Magin Wide-Mouth's song, Hanil High-Brow dreamed she quicked her own belly's eggs with her own eyes' salt. She stood on her head so the dream would tumble from her pate, but she dreamed another down-up dream. She dreamed her eggs were in her eyes and her belly was seeded with salt. And waking or sleeping she was strange after that.

When her egg was ripe next spring, she pulled it from her belly before its time, not even telling her vollow-mate Kalen. She would have buried it under the sand, left it to dry-death, for fear her dream be troth. Yet the quaver of her fearing shook loose tears; her own tear fell on the egg to quick it.

She laid it in the vollow of Mar-i-nar and Huven, two old wives who could not lay. For many a spring, they had nursed fry of dreams, piling their vollow with feathers. And the warmth of the feathers cossetted Hanil's egg. Soon a fry kicked through the shell, though Mar-i-nar and Huven had no milk; they fed the fry on chewed-up fish, like a baby gull. Frela Fast-Heart, they called her, for the quickety bird-beat in her breast. And Frela grew slender-fingered hands on the tips of wings. She knew our speech, but she sang *scronse scronse* from a beaky mouth. Her head was feathered, her breast was feathered, and feathers grew down to the ankles of her pretty woman's feet. In her belly grew no eggs, and Frela was racked by a hunger. She watched with her wee darting eyes to steal the eggs of gulls and of galiven bolden too.

"No," cried Hanil, "no. I won't see my daughter lurking eggs."

Against a rough stone she sharpened a feather Frela had dropped. She put out her own eyes.

After the blood she saw white dark, as from within an egg. And her vollow-mate Kalen found poor Hanil wandering the shallows, calling for the slukie to take her.

Kalen took up the bloody feather and hid in rocks above the vollows, waiting for Frela to swoop and lurk. And Kalen pounced on Frela and jabbed the pointed feather shaft into her heart. Frela fell then, her bird tongue quivering, fell on the seaweed mounding the tideline. Kalen tied her up with kelp-braid ropes. She pulled the point from Frela's wound and stanched her blood with kelp-rot slime. Then, spreading Frela's legs, she shoveled her empty egg-place full of sea salt the sun had been drying at the tideline.

"Now do you carry between your legs more seed than ever women carried in pockets under eyes," said Kalen. "This is the troth of Hanil's dream."

Kalen untied Frela then. And Frela went gentle, her wing-tip hand in Kalen's hand. And Kalen brought Frela to Hanil, who crouched in the reeds with her wits loose-gathered.

"Your dream walks the ground," said Kalen, stroking Hanil's hair.

"Oh, is it Frela who brings that fluttering sound, that hissing, like the sea but softer?"

"The land wind roughs my feathers and smooths them," Frela croaked, speaking as one of us at last.

"O daughter," sighed Hanil. "Forgive me. Mine was the treason breeding yours."

"Twice my mother," Frela crooned, "weep no more. I carry in my egg-place the seed of the sea."

And though Hanil's voice was weak and her heart fluttered, she launched her glad-song brave from her throat. She thought a blessing was falling, a cloak, around her; it was her death, numbing first her limbs then her heart.

To honor Hanil all the band turned their backs to the salt-mother sea.

"We will never turn around," they cried.

And the wind blew their tear-wet hair across their faces, spiriting away their eye-horded seed.

When the wind calmed, the bolden touched their fingers to the tear-trails drying on their faces and eyed each other askance. To honor Hanil there was no turning back to Selukilim's sea, yet how would the eggs be quicked if all their store of salt had been wept in grief?

Oh, Frela was the living strength of Hanil's down-up dream! For Frela had only to tighten her belly to spray salt seed through her flute on the eggs. Whenever ripeness swelled them, the wives called for Frela. And alone Frela carried the seed, for none were born of her like her.

The bolden shoveled the vollows further and further inland. Now they named themselves the laundset, growing sleek on rabbits and mice. Only Frela was restless, drawn to chase in wind. Far from the vollows so the fall of her shadow would not stop hearts, she soared and swooped as days followed days. Days followed days. Frela slowed and Frela whitened, then her fast heart stopped. She fell from the sky in mid-swoop, far from the vollows. And before the smuggy mates could rouse, her flesh had been stripped by the scurrit ants. And so the wives found only Frela's bones, ranged in her fallen shape in the grass, feathers blowing around. And *now* how would they quick their eggs?

"Oh, would we had not wept all our tears for Hanil," cried the laundset. And they did not bury Frela's bones, but sat around them holding their breaths, growing thinner.

Before the teeth of Frela's mourners fell from their jaws, Hurle Six-Toes keened a dream. She dreamed they played on flutes of Frela's hollow bones, and the song-motes fell on the ground and quicked it. Soon the fry pushed their heads between crumbs of soil, their hands unfolding like leaves. When they had pushed up taller than grass, they bent down to pull their feet from earth, biting through long, strong heel roots.

All these young ones had a hollow bone, like a flute, between their legs, and on it played seed-songs to quick eggs. They had neither slitties nor feathers but were smooth as seeds.

"Now are seed-salt bearers legion!" cried Hurle to Hrothal Knob-Knee, her mate.

And Hurle's dream became the song the galiven laundset lived. When the bellies of the women ripened, the root-cut seed-bearers blew their salt right into the women's bodies, without waiting for the eggs to drop, so eager were they. And the young grew inside their mothers and were hatched very large, without shells, half of them galiven laundset, half of them root-cut seed-bearers.

Now while the young were growing inside, the laundset mothers slowed to waddle. Fat bellies spread above thin, weak legs. The mothers' slitties hung in folds, and their eyes grew wider, more fearful and dimmer, like the eyes of prey. All the while the seed-bearers hardened, their eyes narrowing.

"They are less like us than Frela," Hurle whispered in Hrothal's ear. "They roam the grass and do not choose mates. They plight their troth to the band of their own, eating all in a ring, and do not close their eyes when they sleep."

And the mothers breathed fear of the seed-bearers marching out in ranks, their faces grim, carrying sticks and stones and calling themselves the truest laundset. They did not catch rabbits and mice in their teeth, but smashed their heads. Sometimes they brought in the meat of creatures no one had dreamed yet, creatures which had no name but *food*, though the mothers waited for dreams to name them *the thunderers, the long-legged*.

As the seed-bearers ate, they looked into air at what was not. Their square, even teeth ground steadily. The mothers shuddered. The grinding of the seed-bearers' teeth filled the air like the noise of a huge engine, though there were no engines anywhere in all the world then, were not even knives of stone. The lewd sameness of the grinding chewing battered the ears of the laundset mothers writhing in their vollows, and they covered their ears, crying "Doom knell."

But no doom covered them; only a shiver walked down their spines on soft, newborn feet at the very moment far away that a crack appeared between earth and sky, as if the world were a hatching egg. And the moon edged away from her vollow near the earth, and turned to us her bright back. And all the eggs of the world separated inside their shells, yolk and white, and the water shunned the embrace of land; rocks and trees, grasses and freshets, gullies and crags drew back from each other, so they were ever so slightly shrunk into their oneness, as if they had been made each alone in the allness of the world. And then like a tide returning, the mothers felt once again the salt water welling in the sockets under their eyes. And they cried out to Selukilim, first of salt and seed and sea, but she was far, far away. Oh, she was lost in the past.

BANDA

You may have imagined them under the bed or flattened in coloring books, but bandas live in forests like other bears. In books they are pictured in smocks and caps; in the forest they wear their fur. Small and round, with toes but no feet, they toddle along on their hind ankles, tilting from one to the other, using their front ones as hands. Their round eyes never blink and have no pupils; their noses twitch over smiling mouths without teeth.

In summer bandas shamble through sunlit thickets popping berries in their mouths. They sing "Rum tiddly rum pum" and "Ho fa the lark." They watch for children who stray from paths, parting briars to pick the berries they drop in their baskets. The bandas worry about the witch, the witch in the hut in a clearing in the tangliest thicket.

"Rum pum ho hum dee-dee deedly dee," sings a banda perched in the crotch of a tree. "O child come up in the tree with me. Do not leave the path to walk through the patches of sun that nest in the needles and leaves on the floor of the forest. The air is darkening around you. Soon the patches of sun will fade; you will be drawn to the yellow windows of the witch's house. She is waiting for you with milk and toast. With her bare hands she stirs the fire beneath the oven. Her forty scrag-tailed cats are bringing her poisonous mushrooms to feed the fire, their eyes as blue as the hearts of the flames.

"When your tummy is round with milk and toast and you sleep by the fire, the witch will spear your heart with the toasting fork and the cats will purr. She will spread your limbs on a cookie sheet and poke her thumbs in your eyes. She will turn your eyes to holes and then your nose. She will braid your hair in thousands of braids of three hairs each that stick up around your head. She will tie the ends with bits of string she has pulled from the nest of a bird."

(She has. She has. The banda knows. He saw her do it. The twigs and straw of the nest fell apart without the string. The eggs fell onto the ground and splattered. The witch turned her back on the cries of the parents. She caressed the strings and licked her lips. "Cookies," she said, "yum tiddle yum.")

Bandas whisper all these things to every child who continues to saunter from thicket to clearing, leaving the path to kick the pine cones, eating the berries he drops in his basket, staining his face and hands, staining his jumper and stockings, drawing nearer the witch's house as the darkness falls. Every time a child wanders without so much as a glance toward the tree where a banda is singing "Rum tum pie," the banda cries.

His tears are not salt but honey, the honey of violets, honey from puddles that collect in the pockets under his eyes. The sticky tears of crying bandas drip in the hair of wandering children. And the tears of bandas save them. Sometimes.

The witch has trouble braiding the hair of a child the banda has cried on. She cannot separate the strands and her fingers stick to each other. The child may awaken before he is baked, awaken blind, his eyes seeing inward. Then he will remember the "Rum tum tiddley," the whisper he heard from the trees. Lying on the cookie sheet, the child may reproach the banda his soft, soft voice, but the banda cannot help it. He has no vocal cords in his throat and his tongue is velvet. No wonder the child thought the banda's whisper was leaves, restless in wind. Still. The banda did the best he could. And does his best as the child wakes up and cries to him, "Why did you not sing louder?"

Sitting in the branches of the tree outside the window, the banda weeps his self-reproach. "Oh why diddle die," says the banda, "why did I not sing loud?" The banda feels so sorry he does not think of himself. Oh dear.

The cats have seen him. They hiss and spit. The witch pulls open the window and out they run. They tear up the tree the banda cries in, but he is sitting near the very top on a twig so thin it would not support a bird. The cats can never reach him. The twigs crack. Cats fall. Their yowling is terrible. The banda's round ears cup the sound, but it does not move him. Still he sings, "Rum tum tee-dum, why diddle die." His tears fall in the cracks between his toes and he licks them up. He thinks his toes are crying. Truly bandas are confused. Their hearts are large, their ears are large, and their stomachs are small, so they are kind, but oh their brains are mostly air. They want to help but cannot remember anything but songs for long. Oh dear, oh dear.

The child waking up on the cookie sheet must lose no time. He must stop reproaching the banda. That will do no good. He must not take the milk and toast the witch is offering once again. He must not ask for his clothes, which the cats have torn to shreds with their claws. He must step off the cookie sheet and walk, using the sheet as a shield, toward the door. Then the spell will be broken. The light from the fire of the oven will be reflected from the cookie sheet back into the witch's eyes. She will be dazzled. The fire in her heart will be drawn to the fire beneath the oven. She will step into the oven, and then the child can slam the door. The witch will burn, making a smell of dirty butter. When the yellow-green smoke curls from the edges of the oven door, the child will see it. His eyes will be bright and round in his head once again. His nose will be the good dear lump it was. He will be wearing his very own clothes, and they will be clean. The child must not stop to unbraid his hair or to pet the cats which fawn around his ankles. One of the cats may turn to a witch if he does. What he must do is take the birch switch from the shelf by the door. If he but touches with the switch each of the cookies standing around the room, the cookies will turn back to children. They will all be wearing their own dear clothes. They will all have their dear round noses, their bright glad eyes. But it will not happen. It never does.

The child will continue to reproach the banda. The child will take the milk and toast. The child will ask for his clothes. Once again he will eat and drink, once again his tummy will round and he will sleep. Again the witch will spear his heart with the toasting fork, and this time the child will not wake up. He will go in the oven. Blue smoke will curl from the edges of the oven door and out of the chimney. The banda in his tree will know then. He will stop singing. He will shinny down the tree and gallop on his ankles through thicket and clearing to the heart of the forest. And though it is early—summer still—he will hibernate, curling in a hollow log or under the root of a tree.

He is not fat enough for this forgetting. He should not sleep now. But he does. He sleeps and dreams and forgets the children the way they were. He cries in his toes and licks them. Sooner or later he wakes, the hair between his toes licked off, surprised at the look of his pale pink skin. He wakes in winter to the sound of children calling each other's names.

Children in snowsuits lie in the snow and move their arms to make angels. Angel after angel. How they love to make them. They make of the path a path of angels, then they must look for patches of clear fresh snow. Farther and farther they go in the forest, looking for clean white space. They are sure to find some. The witch has cleared the fallen branches that poked through the snow and swept spaces clean with a broom of invisible straws. The spaces are just the right size for a child to make an angel in. "Angel rings" the children call them.

The banda in winter is weak. He cannot help the children who are running from angel ring to angel ring, waving their arms above their heads as they lie in the patches of bright clean snow. The children will approach the witch's hut when the air purples to evening. They will love the yellow windows even more than in summer. They will drink the milk and eat the toast and go in the ovens and the banda will not even sigh. It is not the season for that.

The banda is hungry and tired of tears. There are no berries or violets for him to eat. He would starve were it not for the pity of the parents, the mothers and fathers of the birds who were never born, who splattered in their eggs when the witch pulled the strings from the nests. The parents have not flown south with the other birds. All this time they have not gone far from the places where their eggs fell. Their footprints ring the snow that covers these places.

The sorrowing parents pity the ribs of the banda. They think he grieves with them. They beg him to clear the snow from the places where the eggs fell. The banda always demurs. He is polite. But the parents persist.

They are dying, they chirp. They should have flown south. Their tiny hearts that beat so fast cannot beat fast enough to keep out the cold.

"Oh oh oh," says the banda, and puts as many parents as he can in the pockets where his legs join his body. With parents to snuggle in his hip joints, it is awkward for the banda to dig in the snow till he finds the smears of egg on the ground. But he does. He bends his face to the smears of egg and licks them up. "Rum tum tiddle," he sings to himself. He was hungry. The egg is good. He is warm with the birds at his joints and his heart is soaring with the flight the birds did not take south. Then the banda thinks of other bandas, bandas of the opposite sex.

Hidden in the fur of the male's belly is a tiny sprout that blooms in winter like an early crocus poking its head through snow. "Rum dee dum dee dum," sings the male. A female banda is never far away. Hidden in the fur between her legs is a tiny flower. It is a lovely purple color, like the violets she had been eating all summer. "Rum tiddle tiddle," she sings. She is wandering through the snow like the male, bloom in her belly and flight in her joints, licking egg from her lips.

When bandas mate they do not embrace. If they did they would drop the birds in the snow, and their hearts will not permit them. Arms stiff at their sides, they rub their shiny black noses together. Their toes turn in and their bellies poke out. The flowers in the fur of their bellies seek each other. The bandas mate singing "diddle diddle diddle diddle dee dong."

In spring the baby bandas are born. They live in the nests of the birds their parents have wintered in their hip joints. The birds raise the bandas with their own young, feeding them violets and berries instead of worms.

If the witch tries to pull the string from the nest of birds who are raising a banda, she will get no string. The baby banda spits violets and berries onto her hands, staining them the color of blood. She cries out. She goes home. Later she realizes the blood is not hers. It comes off on her cats when she tries to pet them, and they bite her. She tries to wash the stain from her hands, but it only comes off on her cats or on her nose if she happens to scratch it. The witch spends days, even weeks, scrubbing and rubbing to no avail at the stain on her hands. Of course it wears off in time. But all the while she was rubbing and scrubbing, she baked no children and pulled no strings from nests.

If it were not for the baby bandas, you may be sure, there would be far fewer birds and far fewer children everywhere in the world.

DADDY'S IBBIT WIFE

The ibbits thumped and woggled beyond my sheep, but they're gone now. The burrows have crumbled, the mounds are grass-grown. No one knows where the ibbits went, though my wife Turquoise has heard of wild, shy Indians up in Canada who hide from strangers in abandoned burrows. Only the wind in the burrows beyond my sheep, whistling and wheezing like an ocarina player whose fingers aren't quite big enough to cover the holes. And sometimes when the wind plays over the ruined burrows, the coyotes gather and howl, as if one of my lambs had stumbled and fallen, but my lambs don't fall down those holes, nor do the Indians' nor even the Bar-B lambs. Near the burrows, coyotes never catch lambs.

Beyond the burrows—Bar-B range. The Bar-B boys used to tether their horses and creep through the grass to spy on the ibbits, laughing because those big hoppity, pockety, long-eared creatures looked like twelve-year-old girls with big derrieres. Then one day the Bar-B boys saw a genuine twelve-year-old girl out there, naked and with long, tangled hair. When they stopped gaping and scratching their heads, they lassoed her. They brought that gamey little girl into Fort Yebichai, where the white women gave her to the Indians camped around the palisade, claiming she was too savage to be Christian.

Some of the squaws staked the ibbit girl where the free-running dogs could circle and sniff and bark. They gave her a blanket to warm herself, but she dug a hole and warmed herself in her own breath, hiding from the dogs.

The Indians gave her suet pudding, jerky, venison, bacon, but gaunt as she was she wouldn't eat meat or meat fat. She dug up roots and tore at grass, though chewing it was grinding down her teeth. The Indians brought her corn cakes, and she ate those all right.

After she saw the dogs wouldn't go for her, just steal her food, she stopped pulling on her tether. And the Indians gave her a bit of mirror, so she could see she was like them, but she cut herself on its edge, so they took it back.

Then their doctor, Shawatee, Coyote Walks Sideways, slapped on her chest a daub of mud tufted with ibbit fur. He shook his rattles and sang, trying to exorcise her heart of demons. He was hopping and chanting, his gourd making chatter like seeds rattling down an ibbit tunnel. And she rose from where she was curled around her water dish, started dancing too, which wasn't the Yebichai way. The sick one's supposed to lie there moaning.

Some say Shawatee untied her and she bolted down into their church house underground. (You won't see that house—it's gone now. No one left to tend it.) Others say Shawatee and the girl were dancing like creatures never before seen on earth. Then Shawatee took her home where Spotted Pony, his wife, could teach her how to plant corn, weave baskets—all the work those women did. Shawatee covered the girl with one of Pony's dresses, but the girl turned her face to a wall. When Spotted Pony brought her poisoned water, she ran outdoors, thumped on the ground, and hundreds of coyotes came and sat around the Yebichai camp, their eyes a ring of fire. The Indians shook with fever, like they'd seen worse than death.

They sent some wise old men to the chief of the post, Major Reeves. "That girl is white," said the old men. "You whites must take her."

So the major put the ibbit girl right in jail, though the jail was for men. The jailer had never before locked up a female that wasn't a whore. The ibbit girl circled her cell shaking her bars, tore her blanket to shreds and dug herself under the shreds to fret, her dress flipped over her head.

Someone was watching from the next cell.

"That's sweet," he said to himself, eyeing her stuck-up rump. The jailer didn't even look—busy with an illustrated newspaper.

"Pssst!" said the drunk in the tank next to hers—that drunk was my father, Clemens Catton.

She didn't even look up.

"Hey! Miss! Look to your thank-you-kindly."

"Keep it down," hollered the keys.

Lily (that was not her name yet)—Lily sat up. She knew no English, but the noise had roused her. The dress fell down around her privates.

"Better," muttered Daddy.

Her squatting on her blanket rags, her forearms on her haunches, peering all around—every once in a while she reached up a foot, scratched behind an ear. Daddy began to wonder whether she was human. He sat on his bunk, tried to get his foot behind his own ear, but his joints were too stiff. Maybe she was human, maybe she wasn't. He just lay back and watched her. And Keys looked up from his paper now and then, laughing.

"What's to come of her?" Daddy asked.

"That's what they're trying to figure," Keys replied. "She don't know the business end of a broom. She can't talk, read, write or count her change. Got some funny ways with eats and ain't house-broke. She don't belong in town, but we can't leave her out there."

"I'll marry her," Daddy said.

"You'll—"

"Marry her. I haven't got much, but she won't want much. She'll have a roof and a bed."

"She ain't a woman yet."

"She'll grow."

"Seen her eat?"

"Grass is cheap."

The truth is, Daddy didn't care what she ate. He was already scheming to sell his saddle and his .45, get an old wagon, paint on the side, Wild Woman of the Prairie.

They'd stop outside a town, he'd dig her a hole, pile a mound nearby. All he had to do to get her going was stamp his foot, then she'd undle and slap, and the tip would clap and throw money. If any man tried something funny, Old Clem ran him off with his Winchester.

"This girl's grub," he said.

He had named her Lily after Langtry, whose picture was in the illustrateds. She would come when he called, though at first he didn't call much. Even after her breasts swelled, he slept outside her stuffy little box of a wagon. Then he saw her whimpering, which kept him awake, was from sleeping alone, so he sawed out a window and moved his bedroll in. When we young came, we slept there too.

He had some time raising us, yakking how we were not to eat with our hands like our mother, but from a plate with a fork, like him. Nesters would nag him to put us in school, but we didn't want to stay indoors. He taught us to write our names. And Mommy taught us too, her dance talk. We always knew what she meant, and we'd tell Daddy, "More beans, more cornbread."

And we understood not just her wants, her needs, but her reminiscences.

"She says the sisters are watching the babies, the brothers looking old Tooth Eyes Coyote straight on, scaring him with the thought of his own teeth."

"Oh wind whistle," Daddy would say. "She never said any such thing, wiggling her fanny and kicking, twitching her nose like she had whiskers."

We'd show him what she meant by this little hop and that little wiggle. And he began to be able to read her. He could have wiggle-talked and thump-spoke with her, but he refused.

"Show *her* how to speak," he groused. "Tell *her* she's human—after all, she can *see*."

Now he had a point there. She was always looking way off, and ibbits saw near if at all from their pink-slit eyes. If the wind was right, you could come right up on their twitching noses and quivery whiskers. The sisters would pick up acorns in the pads of their feet, drop them in their pouches, think they'd picked up their young. Daddy told us Mommy must have crawled from a nester's hut as a babe, been stuffed in a pouch by mistake. We asked her, in foot-speak; she actually laughed, a hoarse chuckle, a bubble of mirth from the belly, like anyone. She didn't believe she was human, though. She wouldn't talk, and she couldn't talk. Daddy looked down her throat, to see her vocal cords, and found them shrivelled to hairs.

Mommy always danced the same tale, beginning with Tooth Eyes, slithering into a village on his belly, the ibbits popping down their burrows, digging further and further under till they came to a big dirt room where they bit each other's fleas and licked each other clean. Deeper in the earth, in a tunnel no longer known, was an old, old mother, her pocket stretched big enough for all the babies, all the full-grown, even the fading. They could all crawl in to drink milk, while the big old mother told how the dead get reborn to a world where day is night; how the tooth eyes dream there are no more burrows; how the dead need no burrows, Tooth Eyes's dream for them is true.

The big old mother tells the ibbits the names they'll wear in the world of the dead. There, they'll be known, not by their smells, but by their looks. Each one will wear a different mask, and many sounds will come from their mouths. The sisters will have no pouches; their children will be born with no place to hide. All their dead days will pass, wind-swept and light-struck, in houses above the ground. Not even tunnels between the houses. The big old mother says the dead settle far apart and peer at each other from long distances, forgetting each other's touch. Even when they share their secrets they're not cherished, so alone are they in their skins. But, swears the mother of mothers, if one could make them listen, the dead might all give up their souls to send just one among them back to life.

One night we were running a torchlight meeting. One of my brothers was beating a tambourine, Daddy was calling, "See the genuine wild-heart woman," I was taking quarters in a hat, a white-haired man said, "I'll pay extra. We'd like to talk with her privately." And he gestured at a white-haired woman with an iron-hard mouth. I led them over to Lily's mound.

"Eliza?" asked the woman.

And Lily started shaking, her eyeballs two white rings around the blue.

"Remember your cradle in the back of the Conestoga?"

Lily just rolled on her back and whimpered.

They looked at each other and nodded, then turned to go. They could see she was no longer theirs, or if she was, we dirty-footed brats came with her.

"Won't cost more to see her dance," I said.

They didn't want to watch any exhibition.

We shrugged. Other folks were waiting. Daddy went to Mommy, who was trembling like winter had claimed her bones.

"Lily," said Daddy, taking off his hat. "My luck had never been good; with you I thought it would change, and it did, but I got joy, too, which I had never known, and I'm grateful to you—grateful, M'am."

She just watched him. She didn't know, or maybe she did, but knew no way to make him know she knew. Then for the very first time he thump-spoke. They had some foot-chat between them. Soon enough he shook his head.

"What's she saying?" he asked me.

I suppose I looked at him funny.

"She says she belongs with you, Daddy. She just wishes we weren't all dead."

Now she thump-spoke her run from Shawatee to the church house. Down the ladder to the first floor, where they stored the rattles, masks and feathers, then down another ladder. There, Yebichai men talked deeds—when to plant, when to war and feast and dance. They smoked pipes there; the room was black and foggy. She moved on down through the swirls of smoke to the floor where the boys slept, waiting to be changed to men. They dozed without eating or drinking till they dreamed the names that would change them, but she couldn't breathe that air all thick with names. She went down to the floor where the bridegrooms fasted, praying to open the doors to their wives' bodies. This floor smelled lazy and peaceful, like honeymoon sleep, but she was drawn on down.

Beneath the bridegrooms' floor the warriors danced themselves to lather, drinking corn liquor and eating the root tips of blue-red grass. They bit off their own fingers if they didn't meet their enemies soon. They had eyes in their teeth, like coyotes. They snarled at Lily as she slid, panting, into the lowest room, the sixth and last, tunnels branching into earth like roots. There sat a withered old sister with the feet and legs of a human, the face, paws, and ears of an ibbit, her pouch full of dead men and women growing fur. Long ears pushed from the sides of their heads; whiskers sprouted from their cheeks. When their bellies pouched, they hopped away through the tunnels. Lily had one foot in the old crone's pouch when Shawatee pulled her back.

After the white-hairs' visit, Lily danced harder than ever, sometimes dancing all night, by herself, in the moonlight, while Daddy tossed and turned in the wagon. And one night she danced herself dead—that's all, dead.

Daddy put on his good shirt, went to the preacher and the undertaker, hat in hand. They hemmed and hawed, so Daddy went to old Shawatee; he took her body down in their church house like they did then. Daddy hung up his shirt, uncapped a bottle and drank himself to death within a year. I gave him to Shawatee, too—let the tongues of the blue-eyes clack and waggle in the wind that blows across this land I bought with what little money Daddy left, tied in a sock. I run these sheep and look over the mound where the church house was, to the old ibbit village, all the time thinking. Lambing, shearing—it's a life.

Now once I asked Turquoise—Shawatee's granddaughter—why our sheep always have enough grass; the Yebichai sheep sure don't. She said I was my mother's son.

"But Lily was human and never kept sheep."

"They don't distinguish."

Turquoise said an ibbit looking in one of our mirrors would see a human. And when Lily looked in the mirror the Yebichai gave her, she saw an ibbit.

"Why don't we see ibbits when we look in mirrors?"

"You do," said Turquoise.

She leaves squash and beans out by the ibbit holes. She says we owe for our sheep, which are watched.

"But who watches?" I've said. "There's no one there, and ibbits never could see with their pink little eyes."

She said the dead who didn't get to Canada—that's right, the dead who didn't make it.

YIQH-YAQH

(Ying-Yang, Y'ikq-Yagh, Y'Shi'Yah)

These dark and light horses with feet like goats and horns in the middle of their foreheads live in the fastnesses of Thok Nang, a small domain surrounded by Tibet and claimed by the Urdhiar tribe. An observer would say the beasts are striped, but a yiqh-yaqh is two beasts, a light horse caught in a dark cage and a dark horse caught in a light one. Neither can escape.

The light horse sleeps by day and runs by night; the dark one runs when the light one sleeps. The light eats the berries that grow on the slopes of Mount Thign'at; the dark eats a moss that grows in the shadow of Thign'at.

The light forget they have stood in the valley, swishing the flies from each other's faces. The dark forget they have licked the mountaintop ice from each other's flanks. Neither remembers they have danced with hooves on each other's shoulders, horns chiming like bone necklaces hung in a doorway. The changing mares butt their foals away from their bellies.

A foal is born with no horn but with three eyes, one in the middle of his forehead. With this sleepless eye, the foal can sometimes spot the leopards stretched on rocks. As he grows to a colt, surer-footed and sharper-hooved, the eye clouds then hardens to an ivory knob that grows into a thin, sharp horn which falls when the animal is old, leaving a star-shaped scar.

Some Urdhiar believe the horns grow because the horses tire of third eyes that never sleep. "It is too much seeing," they say. Others say the horn is itself an eye, long and pointed to discern what is hidden. Because the horns are so hard no ordinary person can carve or break them, the Urdhiar believe that possessing them protects against enemies. The horns are valued for their power, then, and because they are difficult to come by.

Summer is long in the dark-horse valley; flowers carpet its floor, and their pollen makes the Urdhiar sneeze. On three sides the valley floor abuts steep cliffs. The fourth side abuts a boulder field so treacherous even the leopard fears it. Only the yiqh-yaqh crosses, trotting over the boulders with hooves clicking and sliding.

Greatly as the Urdhiar dislike "the valley of the myriad nuisances," they dislike the mountain highlands more. There the air is hard to breathe, and ice makes passage difficult. The summit of Mount Thign'at is so far from earth not even the light-horse yiqh-yaqh climb to it. The Urdhiar ancestors live at the very top—the faithless ones who have mated with the leopard. With their six-headed feline offspring, they stalk the light horses cantering over the snow fields. They stalk the boys preparing for manhood who follow the yiqh-yaqh day and night, sleeping little and eating less—a quest and a watch that may last for years. A boy hopes to catch a horn as it falls from an aging yiqh-yaqh's forehead, polish it and set it into his helmet.

Some of the Urdhiar men never leave off questing, though they have long since horned their helmets and taken wives. In the long evenings of the short summers, they do not join the fermented-milk drinkers bragging and lying. Like the boys they were, these lonely men follow dark horses up from the valley, watching for the horns to fall. Some of them sleep with hundreds of horns piled beneath their heads. They claim they are vouchsafed ancestor dreams to make them agile and canny. Truly, when the yiqh-yaqh catchers descend to the valley in early summer, noses plugged with barley paste, the dreamers are the fastest on the ropes.

The catchers raise the dark horses in large rope baskets and carry the baskets home on pairs of poles. There the dark horses eat moss from the hands of children. They stand in the fields all day long, stamping their feet and swishing their tails to ward off flies, keeping the crows from the yield of the barley.

When captive dark horses, like the free, turn light each dusk, they must be moved for the night lest they trample the barley, but they cannot be tethered among the herds of ponies kept by the Urdhiar. The fierce light-horse screaming would panic the ponies. They would pull their stakes from the ground and follow the yiqh-yaqh up to the highlands, there to be lost. So before nightfall herders lead the captive yiqh-yaqh to a pen not far from the ancestor shrine, on the lower slopes of Mount Thign'at.

The herders tell no one—certainly not their wives—where the pen is. Sometimes, on a foggy day, the men themselves forget and are lost. They fall asleep on their feet and are led by their yiqh-yaqh to the top of the mountain, where the faithless ancestors' six-headed leopard-children eat them, drinking their blood from their skulls. When the bones of the herders' bodies have been gnawed clean, the six-headed children crack them and suck out the marrow, then burn them in the invisible fires which flare in the heart of snow.

"The wickedest murderers would have left us the bones," moan the victims' kin. "Without the bones to polish as beads, how will the wives of the lost ones remarry? How will their daughters find husbands?"

And they ring their eyes with soot and wail in the doorways.

The Urdhiar live in windowless dirt-floored houses of stone on the plain where they raise their barley and run their spotted ponies, which they are always stealing from one another. In summer the ponies are tethered on the grassy plain night and day. In winter they are stabled in the houses at night but tethered by day in the stubble of the barley, where they paw through the snow for gleanings.

The Urdhiar reserve the harvested barleycorn for themselves—all but the seed corns—cooking it to a paste and mixing it with butter, then dropping balls of it into barley beer, pony-mare's milk, pony blood, or even (on caravan journeys when the pony hide canteens are dry) pony urine.

The Urdhiar will not eat pony meat, not even if they are starving. Only a crazed Urdhiar will eat the flesh of any animal or suck the yolk from any bird's egg, and if he is discovered, he is stoned. Yet no Urdhiar hesitates to strip the hide from a dead pony. The hides and hairs of ponies are traded, hoarded, given and used for every conceivable purpose. All of the garments of men—their tunics, leggings, and penis sheathes—are of pony skin; their long hair is braided and tied with thongs of it. Their coats are quilted pony skin stuffed with pony hair. Pony hairs are sewn to the back lower rims of their pony-skin helmets, so pony hair flows in the wind of the Urdhiars' riding above the manes and tails of their mounts. "The hide of the pony is the skin of the man," say the Urdhiar, who believe there is power in clothing. That is why their women wear so little of it—only veils of the most insubstantial silk which are rolled and tied at the waist as the women go about their chores, shaken out and thrown over their heads when strangers visit.

In summer the women are allowed to wear broad-brimmed barley-straw hats. Squatting on their heels to plant the kernels of barleycorn, they grow brown and leathery and muscular. They shake their fists at the circling crows.

When the barley has been harvested, they take one last bath in the crop-water ditches, then stand at sunset on the stone walls that border their fields, unrolling their veils. Each woman swings her veil by one corner around her head, and the sky fills with whorls of color. Then the oldest woman of each household untethers the yiqh-yaqh changing from dark to light in her fields.

"Ya ha!" shout the women.

The light horses head for the mountains.

In winter—forbidden to leave their houses—the women speak in whispers and squint in the smoke of the cooking fires, weaving pony-hair ropes and coiling them into baskets. They wash in the urine of the stabled ponies, which whitens and softens their skin and jellies their wits, so they kiss their husbands' feet and beg them to pull down their penis sheathes.

The men do not bathe all winter, though in summer they throw off their helmets and sluice their heads in the mountain streams, then roll with their ponies. They lie on the banks in loose, wet leathers while their ponies stamp and swish at flies. Before the leathers are dry, the men ride to a dusty hollow where they wallow till they are white as ghosts, their own children do not know them.

Many of the children die before they are grown. Running barefoot in dung, they contract worms which lodge beneath their skin, leaving star-shaped scars, then burrow inward to the lungs. Most Urdhiar are infested. That is why they cannot descend to the valley without sneezing, why they cannot breathe on the mountaintops. The scars resemble the scars on the foreheads of yiqh-yaqh that have shed their horns, and indeed, the Urdhiar distrust the hornless yiqh-yaqh. They believe that to capture one brings a household bad luck; all of its children will die of worms.

When an Urdhiar dies, the relatives chop up the body, breaking the bones to expose the marrow and piling the pieces on the tablelike roof of the ancestor shrine. They pray that crows will come; they believe any leopards finding the flesh will use the understanding gained by eating it to hunt humans. And if the offspring of the faithless dead eat the flesh—ah!—they will slaughter whole villages.

When a pony dies, the Urdhiar skin it, then pile its hacked body parts on the roof of the shrine. And when smut blackens barley, they pile the harvest on the roof. But when a yiqh-yaqh dies, the Urdhiar who finds it buries it in a pit filled with hot ashes, having first stripped off its hide. Woe to him if his wife is pregnant! He must move from his house until she gives birth so the child will not be born deformed. His wife is shut up alone with a several-months' supply of pony dung to burn and barley paste to eat. In winter she sees her husband when he lets the ponies in and out of the house where they are stabled. In summer she sees no one, not even the ponies. She wrings her hands in the dark house, knowing the other women are out in the light, planting the fields and splashing in the ditches.

"Sisters!" she calls. "Sisters! Unbar the door!"

She may pull the hairs from her head, one by one, and lay them on the fire. She may burn her veil and her barley-straw hat. She may thrust her fingers and toes into the fire, calling on the ancestors. No one will help her.

"Dead yiqh-yaqh curse heavy-bellied women in summer, live curse light-bellied ones in winter"—that is an Urdhiar saying. And indeed, when the winter is long, many women rise from their beds to pace among the stomping ponies, patting their flanks and pulling their forelocks. In the morning when their husbands let the ponies out, these women slip out with them. Running through the snow on bare feet, they leave the ponies behind, heading for the trail between the slopes of Mount Thign'at. Sometimes they burrow through drifts higher than their heads, wearing nothing but snow-wet veils that cling as death then stiffen and flap as the women breast the wind.

Not having catchers' ropes to lower themselves into the dark-horse valley, the women tiptoe across the boulder field. Some are buried in rock slides, but others reach the dark horses huddled in a grove. The women stroke the animals' rumps, collecting their urine in stiff hands to rub on their numb white feet. They fling off their veils and whirl, crying "Ha ya! Ha ya! Ha ya!" At sunset they ride light horses up the mountain slopes, where they stay all night, clinging to the horses' shining horns.

Toward morning most of the women return to their villages, stealing into their own houses before the men wake up. But some do not go home at all. They walk barefoot through the snow-filled passes to the walled city where the Urdhiar caravans trade in summer. They remember nothing, not even their names.

In late spring the males of each household draw lots to see who will journey with the catchers to the valley and who with the caravan to the city, where the Urdhiar sell ponies, pony skins, and pony-hair rope baskets, buying veils, knives, meat axes, needles, and the coins the women wear on rings through their ears and noses.

The chief trader of the caravan and the chief roper of the catching expedition are chosen from among those who wear mantles of yiqh-yaqh about their shoulders. In fact *shi-yiqh-yaqh-shah*, the word for chief in Urdhiar, means "he who wears the dark and the light." A man who wears the mantle will take the slippery path and marry the fierce woman; he will overload his ponies and shinny down a fraying rope. Such a man is admired by others, but no man lightly dons the stripes. First he sits at the ancestor shrine, pouring offerings of blood on the altar. Then he sleeps in the shrine house.

If leopards enter his dream to eat barley paste from his hand, he dons the hide in the morning. If the leopards leave the paste but devour him, he smothers the hide in ash when he wakes. Then he buries it, disguising the cache so it cannot be found.

A man who wears the hide may rape the wives, daughters, and sisters of other men. He may demand their best ponies, their strongest baskets, the nose- and ear-wealth of their women, even their necklaces of ancestor bones. His householders must wash his feet and comb his hair and pick off his lice.

When he is so old he cannot control his spittle, he drapes the mantle over the shoulders of his son, who begins at once to demand ponies and women.

If a man lies about a dream to gain the mantle right, his wife mocks him, throwing her legs across him and snickering. If he ties her wrists and her ankles with pony-hide thongs, she spits on them to loosen them while he sleeps, then binds his wrists and ankles. So fettered, he will snore past sunrise. Dressing in his clothes, the yiqh-yaqh mantle over her shoulders, she strides from the house in his place.

The Urdhiar say a woman in a yiqh-yaqh mantle—a jidi—is terrible to behold. She flaps the mantle at foraging ponies and laughs at their panic. She runs from house to house, pissing on cooking fires. While the squatting wives hiss, she smears her dung on their walls. These hapless women will be beaten when their husbands find them fumbling with the bow, string and tinder, trying to rekindle the sodden fires. The jidi will not have stayed to help. As evening falls, she will have headed up the mountain, past the yiqh-yaqh pen. No one will know where she has gone.

Back in the village the men dig each other in the ribs and point to the house where the jidi's husband crouches in a corner without his clothes, muttering at his children who have untied him and clamor for food.

When the jidi returns several days later, she looks the way she always looks, but her eyes have narrow golden circles around the pupils. The yiqh-yaqh mantle is now gold with brown spots. The mane, horn and hooves have disappeared; the tail is the tail of a cat.

"My dishonor is great," says the husband.

"You may beat me," the jidi says.

"I cannot beat you if you give me permission."

"Then I do not give you permission."

Still wearing the mantle, the jidi kneels on the floor. He seizes the pony-hide whip with its seventeen knots, brings it down on her back, and beats her till the blood runs. She does not cry out, nor will she say where she has been. When her husband flicks the mantle with his whip, the tail of it swats his face.

Nine months later the jidi gives birth to a girl who talks from her very first breath. She dreams of leopards with six red mouths, speaking of them in her sleep in a language only her mother knows.

"The six-mouthed leopard stands on the mountain," the mother translates. "He eats his own body, tail first, with his right-most head, then he is a small blue egg. The egg hatches and a blood-red bird flies out, a bird none of us has seen before, with a forked tongue that quivers fast. Perching on my head, he says our daughter is an ancestor now. She must go up the mountain."

Always in the dream the girl must go up the mountain, as her mother, the jidi, has gone before her. The girl's father is aghast. The child is still a toddler, who sways from side to side as she walks. She is too young for a journey—so the father insists. And the mother relents; the girl will make the journey when she has become a woman. And the girl has the same dream every night for many years, until two red bird-tracks appear on her forehead.

"Jalidi," the mother calls her then, "jalidi, daughter of jidi."

Dressed in the jidi's mantle, the jalidi climbs Mount Thign'at alone. When she returns, her eyes have narrow golden circles around the pupils;

she has in her hand a yiqh-yaqh horn. She borrows her father's pony-skin-ning knife and carves barley kernels on the horn, making a penis sheathe which her father snatches at once. Now he has the strength of ten men. He can dance with his knife between his teeth all night. He can break twenty-six ponies in a day. He can strangle a leopard with his bare hands. But the first thing he does is kneel before his wife.

"Your dishonor has been great," he says. "You may beat me."

"Since you gave your permission, I cannot."

"Then I do not give permission."

"I ask for a gift instead. Our daughter is hungry. Permit her to stew and eat your whip."

When the daughter has eaten, she announces her intention to wear men's clothes and never to marry. A special house is built for her near the ancestor shrine. She hangs her father's penis sheathe and her mother's man-tle above its door, lives alone, and cures the sick, her lightest touch drawing starshaped worms from children's lungs. The men bring her all the yiqh-yaqh horns that have been burning desires on the undersides of their eyelids, hoping she will make the horns into penis sheathes, but she never makes a sheathe again. She grinds the horns to powder—all but the tips—and mixes the powder to paste with her spit. She puts the paste into the horn tips and seals these vials with mare's-milk butter. The men take the vials to the city, exchanging them for gold and silver, and the Urdhiar prosper.

The city-dwellers say a potion of powdered horn brings good fortune in love and in the marketplace, but a daughter born to a man who drinks it may run away to the Urdhiar, stealing into one of their houses at daybreak, dropping her clothes behind her. "I have come to you, Sister," she says to the wife in bed. In this way Urdhiar men may acquire a number of wives.

What do the jidi, and later the jalidi, do on Mount Thign'at, where the air is too thin to breathe? Some say the jidi plucks a small red flower that grows in a crack at the very top of the mountain. In the flower is the seed that fathers the jalidi. Others say no flower could survive the year-round snow at the top of the mountain. They say the jidi copulates with the faithless ancestors, one by one, thousands of them, and the jalidi copulates with the children of the faithless by leopards, many more thousands, cold and white as their ghostly parents, but with leopard-spotted fur and gold-rimmed eyes and six heads. Still others would have it neither jidi nor jalidi copulates at all. Rather they stroke the rumps of the six-headed offspring and catch their urine in cupped hands; they rub it into their eyes.

Some Urdhiar insist the jalidi does not go to the top of the mountain, but to a spring just below the top, a trickle of cold pure water from a crack in a rock. They say she watches the ancestors drinking, a faint movement of air and spray, a shimmer on the rocks like a mirage but near. They say the six-headed offspring drink too, the six pink tongues lapping water in unison, like a dance. And the single-headed leopards drink, and the light-horse yiqh-yaqh—one by one they drink then turn to go down the mountain, while the woman watches motionless on the rock the spring flows from. When all the animals have drunk from the rock, the woman herself drinks, her face dipped into the cold water, lapping like those who have gone before her, pulling water with her tongue into her open throat. And when she raises her head from the spring her eyes are rimmed with gold.

FORRAGO

Now in the darkest and narrowest alleys of Porto Affraia, alleys too dark and narrow even for stand-up whores and small-time thieves, there thrive some small ratty creatures with greasy, ashen coats and greedy big eyes. The teeth of these *fragaos*, or forragos, are sharper than scimitars. With them the 'ragos nibble in the manner of a terrible army carving its way through some meatlike ranks, making row after row of crescent-shaped marks, so 'tis said by the poets the beasts eat in fields of moons. And the people throw in the 'ragos' lairs all the midden of the place, rags of flax and muslin and wool, worn-out harnesses, stems and hulls of grain, ruined oars and rotten planks. Why I have seen them throw in the stinking carcass of a camel dead for a week!

By eating without surcease, and sleeping with their big eyes open, their jaws moving, the 'ragos consume many times their weight each day. They never stop spying out meals, and gobbling without scruple, from the earliest infancy. Indeed the young are born with teeth and grab their mothers' teats and chew. While still in the spasms of siblings' breach, she is trying to save herself, dancing and rolling and charging and shaking, her teeth tearing at her young. Sometimes an old mother has but scars for teats!

Mark you well: Her condition and experience have failed to fan in her miserable bosom the smallest spark of pity for others. Most 'specially she has none for the male of the species—alas! alas! smaller than she—who approaches intrepidly his enormous love all eyes and teeth, drawn by the glamorous musk, a heady brew—I tell you it smells to me like rancid cheese and new-mown hay, like the insides of shoes, and the freshest milk, like a four-day-old fish and a whole field of roses—this musk she sweats to lure him. She attends him demurely, as if she did not know she oozed a powerful, gamey enticement, her little wide-eyed face half-masked between her fore-paws, her steaming buttocks coyly raised, the machine of her jaws moving still.

Watch Little Fellow! Watch! Do not run from hiding till her eyes have closed!

There is his chance, see; her eyes do close for a while.

Not much later the poor little blighter concludes he has taken his pleasure in a tight spot, for his member has swole up to stick him fast. He tugs now more fervently than ever he pushed and pulled, but tug as he will, he cannot withdraw, though her eyes are opening, her head is turning. Full days after she has eaten him tail and ear, his shrunken member falls from her.

And she snaps it up.

You shake your heads; you allow she is evil. And indeed she is remorseless wicked, yet even she enlarges the stock of blessing in this world. Consider the beggar boys who whine and steal and cozzen there, orphan lads, with nary a settled prospect for bread: They trap the terrible 'rago dams in glass jars. Now when the bait is consumed—the finger of an old glove, a toe-nail paring, a strand of hair will do—the damsels' teeth find no purchase. Quite soon they are starved stone dead and their little corpses sold to druggists for a very good price. And when the musk is squeezed from the vicious rumps, an exquisite perfume is refined. It smells like the look of the moonlight falling across the water, a deceptive path a man might drown in were he the fool to yield to its beckoning. I do not recommend it myself. Yet 'tis said a seaman mounting a frail whose earlobes have been daubed with this essence will die consumed by the teeth of bliss, and never once think of his home. And 'tis said that a convicted murderer in Porto Affraia was put to death at his own request by a whore wearing forrago musk. Who would not prefer it to the rope or knife?

MURUMOREN,
OR BREACH AT THE CASTING

excerpt from

The Marvelous Adventures of Pierre Baptiste,
Father and Mother, First and Last
Including His Life, Times, Friends and
Baleful and Voluptuous Beasts

In 1754 an exceedingly valuable slave named Pierre, trained as a bookkeeper, escaped by sea in a rum cask from a sugarcane plantation in the French Anduves. He floated away from the shipping lanes to wash up on the shore of the island we know as Big Cayama, then uninhabited and bearing no name. The cask rode in at high tide and bumped against the shore on the breaking waves for a long time before Pierre dared come out. He was hungry, wet and thirsty; his store of biscuits was exhausted, his canteen of fresh water empty. Yet he shivered in the cask for hours, occasionally uncorking a bunghole and putting his eye to it. He feared, he records in his memoirs*, he had landed on one of the rum-, sugar-, and molasses-producing islands neighboring Saint-Gilbert, from which he had escaped. He feared he would be returned to his master, whipped with a cat-o'-nine-tails, caged in the sun with no food or water until his tongue turned black, then sold to a worse master than Auguste Henri Lemoyne Du Fay, the third son in a cadet branch of the illustrious family.

"My bunghole eye told how the sea had cast me up, not in any populous Spanish port, as I had hoped, but on an island barely inhabited, an island

---

*Discovered in a sea-abraded bottle when excavation commenced for the Cayama Hilton, the *Aventures merveilleuses* were written with gull-feather pens dipped in squid's ink on paper made from pounded palm bark.

resembling Saint-Gilbert, even to the proliferation of orchids. And fearing my escapade would end in comeuppance worse than any I had yet received, I cramped in the cask, and clutching my talisman, a pouch I had had from my mother, I prayed for salvation to the god of the fat white priest and to the gods of my own people, whose names I did not know. The bunghole was on the landward side of the cask and gave no view of the waters, yet I could hear them slapping and murmuring, indeed I could feel the cask shift in the waves and hear the grunt of sand beneath me. I dozed and pondered, dozed and pondered, knowing I would have to leave the cask in search of food and water, yet reluctant to do so.

"'Now I have left behind all I know,' I bespoke me. 'The children black and white running through the dust of the yard, their mothers' voices floating after them, the smell of yam and manioc porridge bubbling in the iron skillets of the quarters. And after dinner the old women gathering children near a fire to tell stories of wives who changed to birds to please their husbands, of husbands who changed to snakes to spy on their wives, of naughty children changed to kernels of grain and eaten by their parents' hens, and of jealous gods who stole the rich men's cows.'

"I feared I would never again hear the old women, and I feared I would, for not to hear them was to be lost in freedom, and to hear them was to have been returned to Monsieur. Oh, I did not want to be caught, to be punished to labor harder than ever in the fields, grinding bones and tearing muscles, planting and hoeing and cutting cane, all too near the library where I had passed so many pleasant hours, ciphering overt and reading surreptitious, tortured by the smell of ink. And then there was the specter of a worse master than Du Fay, the grinning Baron Skull, in his satin waistcoat, whom all the slaves feared.

"The sky having darkened for a second time, I determined to explore the land to which fortune and the tides had carried me, and I peered through the bunghole one more time, to ascertain my safety in emerging. There met my eye then a round yellow one with a black center, the eye, methought, of a frightful large fish. In thoughtless panic, I leapt from the cask, popping its lid, and saw in the dusk an apparition—Madame Du Fay! changed by immersion to a creature of the sea, a metal-haired nereid with frog's feet.

"'Madame,' said I, 'Have you come to chide or left your husband to follow a slave? Foolish woman! To speak plain, you corrupt yourself, and your husband's search will be relentless. Truly I am compromised. I beg you return how you came, but only, I pray you, forbear to reveal me!'

"Her mouth opened and closed in such a manner I saw at once she was dumb. I put out my hand to her, and she hopped a few steps back on her amphibolous feet, her eyes shining. She had no nose!

"After we had stared at each other some time, she disappeared beneath the waves and came not again for days. By then I had circumambulated the island and knew its parts. I had decided the sea shade were a phantasm, a figure of imagining, without a body. I devoted myself to comfortable, necessary tasks, viz: I constructed a hut of driftwood chinked with sea weeds, larger and roomier than my plantation kennel, and with a veranda, like a white man's house. I found a fresh-water spring and fruit trees and was passing content. If I had been able to change my linen and discover some books, I might have accounted myself in paradise, though I did want company and prattled to myself day and night, bidding myself good morrow and good evening and asking and answering questions on all manner of subjects.

"I had become accustomed to finding my company in books, and verily all my discourse had long been with their authors, with whom I continue my conversation even now:

Pintal: At the heart of solitude is sorrow, at the heart of sorrow is bliss: to know thyself.

Me: And surely my particularity were as difficult to ascertain as that of a bird from other parts drawn to a remote sea isle by tempest, a bird unknown to the other creatures of the place who do shun it, a bird that may only suppose it has been hatched from an egg.

"I had stepped into books even as I had once dreamed of stepping into Monsieur's pictures, there to enjoy a universe that is our own in all its perfection. To asseverate the necessity that follows, that Creation were other than perfect, were blasphemy, I am aware, though men and beasts and vegetables and perhaps winds and water do suffer from the uneven distribution of benefits on Earth and in the Heavens. Still the presumption must be honored that our Creator were as skilled, at least, as a watchmaker and did know what parts were needed for the working of the whole. Yet I do think that perception of the delicate truth depends on perspective, and, moreover, that even perfection has its lights and shadows. It is not always revealed in the world with clarity. It has not always the apparency it possesses in Monsieur's paintings, or in the books, the memory of which I had entered.

"In time my hunger for books did translate to a hunger for flesh, so I thought one morning to pare an ebony sapling, to spear fish from the rock outcropping at the westward side of my domaine. Were I to fish by day, I discovered, the sun made me dizzy. I fell into the custom of fishing by night.

"Imagine my discomfiture, one mild evening, to perceive wriggling on my spear point—the madamish sea shade. I had speared her just beneath the shoulder blade, where a species of arm—a long fin with fingers—joined the body. Blood gushed from the hole in her pink-speckled skin, and her gill slits heaved. Ah me! I lay her head in the water, so she could breathe, and stanched with the rags of my shirt the flow of her blood. Still she lay in a swoon. When the sun came up, she would be burned if I did not arch over her a roof of sticks and vines. This I did, and she lay calmly, her gills palpitating in the brine, her eyes gaping.

"As the tide went out, she would no longer be able to respire, so I moved her body, lifting it in my arms to follow the receding waters. At first she struggled in my embrace, but after I had lifted her several times, she lay still, her shanky legs draped over my arm and her head with its coarse-crimped curls lolling on my breast. Only once did she bare her teeth, and then I saw for the first time the double row of needles. I began to bring her bits of fish, pushing them between her jaws with a clam shell for fear she would sink the teeth in my hands. But seeing she took the fish very dainty, I vouchsafed to feed her with my fingers, and found her to nibble very careful. So we got on well, and her wound mended.

"I did not see how I could have confused her with Madame, even granting the farfetched conceit a white gentlewoman is another species than a black male slave; even so, this greenish creature were more foreign a species still, even as a snake is less penetrable in nature than a dog or a goat. *Murumoren*, I named her breed.

"I do not know why I thought of her—and think of her—as 'she,' save that the initial confusion with Madame perplexed my perception thereafter, for she bore no mark of her sex, unless one count her long tarnished locks—not in truth hair, but some bony substance like coral.

"Foreign as this creature was, I came to know her ways, a filip of her feet, fast, as a cat will filip its tail when plagued by a nuisance; or a gaze following my hands when I had a fish. And then I came to know many a place on her scaly skin, and most particular on her forehead, she did shiver upon my touching, moving closer to my hand.

"Upbraiding myself for my fondness, I commenced to call her 'ma bonne amie' and finally 'Amie.' I directed all my prattle to her and wept tears of joy and distress when her wound healed, and she dove beneath the billows, returning only for brief nocturnal visits, to be petted on the forehead, provided the shadow of my spear did not fall across her path.

"In this independence as in her helplessness she gawked at me, seeming quite transported by my babble, but in truth it was the talisman pouch which swung from my neck she did eye. This I discovered when she snatched it and retreated promptly beneath the sea. Perhaps she snatched the bag to repay the wound I had inflicted on her, but to think so were small comfort. Now truly I was marooned on a strange island, left entirely to my own understanding, quite cast away. She did not know how I had clung to the talisman as an orchid to its roots. Yet I did not wither or fade, and Amie made good the debt of life according to her own custom.

"Even though she did not breathe through a nose, she was more than capable of gratitude. She repaid my solicitude with fish, which she brought me already chewed into mush and regurgitated at my feet.

"I would have preferred my talisman be returned, or that the fish be brought me whole, but she could not fathom my revulsion: at last I bade her throw up the fish in a coconut rind, and drank while holding my nose. I found the stew sweet and mild, like a medley of fish and yam.

"One evening Amie spewed into the rind a strange seashell, a small cone which crumbled upon my inspection. Thereupon she emitted a yawp, the first noise I had heard of her, and slapped her feet on the water. She brought no more fish for several evenings.

"When she returned I was hungry, having lost the habit of fishing. I lay on my back then and bade her spit the mush directly into my mouth. She did so willingly, spitting into my maw as well several sharp objects I surmised at once were cones. They crumbled on my tongue and though I did spit out shell bits, and pick them from my lips and from between my teeth, my tongue burned as if stung. I dared not swallow for fear the shells be poisonous.

"After a while the burning subsided. I constricted my gullet to swallow, with no consequence, and my tongue, though swollen, did waggle in my mouth as before, so I passed the evening, according to my custom, in prattling. Consider then my great surprise to wake unable to bid myself good morrow. In vain the fingers of one hand then the other did walk past my lips, sortie between my jaws, and explore the moist cave inside my teeth. Where my tongue had rooted, there poked a stump which by wagging I could cajole to an idiot's speech, being now unable to voice half the words in my lexicon. In my disappointment I failed to remark the lumpiness swelling my cheeks, but lay all day in a damp hollow in the sand, shedding tears. I woke to discover Amie squatting above me, butting me with her forehead to be petted.

"I saw at once she intended to dribble gruel between my lips; though the gruel carry more shellfish to undo me completely, I was too weary and hungry to protest and so parted my lips. There came from my mouth then a faint squalling sound. When I stretched a finger gingerly into a cheek pouch, it warmed to the gentle clutch of one minuscule pair of arms, then another. By careful feints with the finger, I counted four—dare I call them infants?—two in each cheek pouch—and surmised that I was in a condition I had never looked to be in—a condition to which I believe no member of my sex has ever before been brought.

"I parted my lips and permitted Amie to flood my mouth with gruel, forbearing to swallow until by an instinct I had not known I possessed, I surmised my young had drunk their fill.

"I did not sleep in my hut that night, nor any night that followed, but lay curled in my hole by the sea. My cheeks grew very large before I was delivered. At the end of my confinement I could scarce lift my head and relied entirely on Amie to feed me, and the tide to clean out my nest. I was suffused with tender thoughts for the young in my cheeks and often lay with my eyes closed, crooning as best I could with my shortened tongue:

> Ba-wal loo-mah ba-ha-wa loo-a-to
> Ba-wa ha-y-too ba ba-wa loo

"Methought I remembered my mother crooning these syllables before she was sold; mayhap she learned the song from my grandmother, who had been brought from across the world in an open boat with a rope through her pierced ankles—so I had been told by the old, in their stories, stories I now had difficulty remembering—did the king whose wife turned into a monkey lure her with nuts or with bananas?—even as I now had difficulty remembering the names of animals and plants, and the difference between Pintal's idea of faith and Nerf's. To conjure my memories, I mumbled intermittently, wagging my stub of tongue, the names of creatures or passages of Pintal, but the effort was fatiguing, and soon enough I returned to crooning 'Ba-wal loo-ma,' which I could pronounce by feverishly working my lips, a circumstance I found most comforting. Comfort, indeed, I had come to crave.

"Yet though my mouth waxed heavy with young, and I was nearly helpless in this state, prey to whatever vicissitudes of fortune might befall me, and most especially to the caprices of tropical weather—to merciless sun and sudden storm—still did Amie disappear beneath the sea each evening after a brief visit to feed me and be touched in her sensitive places. I feared the young in my mouth would follow her when I cast them, be lost to me as my talisman memories, I not clap eyes on them again.

"One evening when I opened my lips to Amie to receive a stream of gruel, the four offspring jumped from between my teeth and cast themselves into the sand before my face, squirming and squalling in the manner of human infants.

"They were as helpless as any human babes, and indeed they bore the impress of my features, and had the lidded eyes of men, and toes on their feet, and skin like men's, not scales. They had gills behind their ears, 'tis true, but noses as well, and as they were to mature the gill slits were to close. They were fine, lusty black babes, though very much smaller than human children. All four would fit in the palm of my hand. Curiously, they lacked those external organs by which we ascertain gender even in infants, having between their legs neither the stamen of the male nor the sepals and calyx of the female.

"They grew rapidly, and soon toddled. *Jérôme Marie, Léon Cléopâtre, Françoise Marcelline,* and *Émile Honorée,* were the names I gave them at their baptism, with which I proceeded in a Christianlike manner, although I could remember no suitable scriptural texts, nor any suitable texts of the philosophers, but only a comic line of de Vereau's, spoken by Amouradet:

> And so with firm resolve to be brave, and hopeful
> heart, we embark on our noble adventure.

"It must be admitted that these words are not eminently suitable, and do not come from an author of any consequence, but I was bound to eke out the dignity of the occasion with scraps. And indeed were any listening who would contemn my heterodoxy, they had first decipher the amorphous syllables that passed and were shaped by my nub of a tongue. I commended my lads to live as sensibly and kindly and joyfully as they could, injuring no creatures except the need arise to kill for food.

"Jéro, Léo, Framo, and Émlo, as the lads came to call themselves, grew to be as elegant as the youth I had seen reflected in Monsieur's pier glasses, tireless swimmers and divers, merry lads with ready laughs and songs on their lips. By day they romped in the sea and ashore, by night they waited with me for their mother—or was she, or he, their father?—to come with our food. In time other sea shades joined Amie, to spit fish and cones in our mouths and proffer their foreheads for rubbing, and so we prospered as a tribe.

"I gave myself with whole heart to founding a race of new creatures, though my tongue grew shorter with each confinement. I know not what manner of mates were foreseen beneath the waves, nor why the sea shades chose to grace us with cones. I am no Monsieur Du Fay, to confound myself in the painting of pictures, neglecting business at hand. I have occupied myself with rearing my children and their children properly, breeding them up gentle with what manners and learning I could impart without books or an example other than mine own. So my life has gone.

"Yet one line of inquiry it frequently falls on me to pursue, although to no avail, viz: If we of this island are all like us, then where do the sea shades come from? How do they breed? Are they born, or created in some other manner?

"Save that my island is limned in shadow as well as light, and myriad orchids push everywhere, I might sometimes imagine I have stepped into one of Monsieur's drawings, of a species yet unknown, a species only hoped for or wished for or feared. But who the artist is I cannot say, though I can say that the mystery of Creation, this very idea, is gilded for me in contemplative moments with all the awesome apparency of which I have spoken. For even as Monsieur, the artist of surpassing ability, is eccentric, temperamental, and finally pathetic, so the nature of the Creator, the Supreme Artist, if such there is, may be equally unfathomable in paradox beyond 'omnipotent,' 'eternal,' 'omnipresent,' and the other familiar grandiloquent reverence.

"My shadow grows shorter each day now. Casting these reckonings, I desire only to append, my sons have all been born with tongues, and taught to speak, however slurred and indistinct a language, first by me, and later, as my tongue did diminish even further, by siblings or uncles or parents. The faculty of speech dwindles with the loss of the tongue during progressive confinements but sing we can into old age, through vibrating the cords in our throats. Peradventure the tongue itself first attracted Amie; indeed, the merest shred in the mouth will still draw gifts of cones.

"Although I have never exchanged a word with Amie, or any other sea shade, yet some mutual understanding has risen, as witness the floating into my nest on the tide one day, unexpected and unbidden, the talisman, the leathern pouch much rotted by the sea, its contents entirely vanished, but still possessed of its power to quiet my heart.

"For was it not right then the pouch should be empty? Never had I known the true nature or provenance of the feather fetishes, woven grass medallions, and strung teeth my mother had given me, dear as these objects were to me, their mystery so much my own. And the thoughts I culled from Monsieur's books—could these have represented Wisdom? Did I ever truly learn to read, sitting on the branches outside the classroom, the orchids I knocked covering me with pollen, and the bees buzzing around me?

"The hut I built upon my arrival here has long since collapsed, and orchids have covered the mound of rubble. The library thoughts of dramatists and philosophers, romancers, poets and priests, did I ever really penetrate them? And if I did, what light can they cast on my fate, which has diverged, I do believe, from the common lot of mankind? What I have come from is nothing to me compared to what I have become. And yet the sea shades sing my mother's songs:

Ba la ba-ha-to ba-wa-lal.

"Against Monsieur and Madame I bear no rancour, my numerous progeny so great a comfort to me, I need no consolation in vengeance. And who can say how the balance shall be cast? Mayhap the portraits Monsieur has painted, glorifying Creation as discovered in these islands, will redeem him from his viciousness and negligence.

"My children I have bred to observe the fat priest's commandment, 'Love thy neighbor.' They would observe the religion of the talisman if I knew what that religion was. And though I do not think any religion profits by repeated immersion in seawater, I count my children, and their children, as civil as any other creatures, notwithstanding humans, who presume themselves the nonpareil. If this sentiment breach piety, may God, or the gods, or both, forgive me my blasphemy. Amen. Baluwa. Bawato. Let Baron Skull come. It is time.

"The humble servant
of my children,

"Pierre, Mère et Père,
Premier, Dernière."

MEAT SONG

In the early days the grasses grew taller than men; people tied the tops of the blades together for houses, just as birds do now. In the noonday sun, we slept on the cool, hard, dry floors of living grass houses that steamed and baked in light. We listened to our houses swaying around us, talking in our ears and singing in wind, bending low around us, bowing the ripening heads of grain that would soon fill our baskets. Yet though the grass was tall and great, rippling and murmuring till it reached the edge of the world, the daughters of grass were pious and humble, devout in the presence of the bull, the very old, very strong bull, who lived at the heart of the world in his own shade with his wives and his dogs.

He was larger than the largest of the far-off trees at the edge of the world, and he could live as long as any tree. His heart beat slowly, his legs moved slowly, and he ate slowly. Sometimes he stood in one place with a front hoof raised for so long he seemed rooted by his other three feet. The black birds with red and yellow heads nested on his horns, and sometimes a bird built a nest in his ear. The eggs might be laid, the chicks peck through the shells before the bull twitched his ear and shook his head, spilling nest and eggs to the ground. The dogs warmed the fallen chicks between their paws, the birds ate the dogs' fleas—in the shadow of the bull, there was peace.

When a boy first dreamed the smell of women, he traveled alone, without clothes and without weapons, into the heart of grass. His ears were full of salt; his neck, wrists, ankles and waist were wound with his mother's hair; he carried a nutshell, his cup. When he found the bull, he made his bed between the heavy hooves and lay against the earth, ear to the ground, listening. He heard through the salt in his ear the familiar murmuring talk of grass, waves of rustle he couldn't understand. The boy lay a long time without eating, drinking only the rain falling into his cup. The sun rose, the moon rose; still the boy lay in the grass.

All his life he had lain on the earth in his father's house, listening for the sawing of grasshoppers. He had learned to hear a grasshopper chewing a leaf at the other end of his village, yet he could not understand the talk of grass that flowed around him, rising and falling, encompassing and meaningless.

Before he went between the hooves, he had sat before his house, cross-legged, like a seer, stroking with grass brushes his drum of bull hide. He had echoed the voices of grass with his brushes of grass, stroking his drum which was wound with strands of his mother's hair, cut at the root when he was born, saved to wrap his neck, his wrists, his ankles, his waist, to make his body a drum, to be brushed with grass when he went between the hooves. Now he was between the hooves, listening, the voices of grass brushing his ears. Still he heard nothing but a swish and a rustle, waves of echoes. Back in his village his brothers were sitting cross-legged before their father's house, playing their drums. Between the hooves, the boy heard echoes and waited.

In the bull's own time, he lowered his head to the boy's. He stretched his long black lips and licked the salt from the boy's ears. He spoke to the boy, a ticklish series of chuckles, clicks, nose-bumps and moans. The boy longed to laugh, but as he had lain on the earth of his father's house, his sisters had tickled his ears with feathers; he had learned to be still. Now the bull tickled his ears a long time; no one knows how long. The boy could not keep count.

"Forty days the earth in my face, forty nights the mouse in my ear," sang his brothers as they drummed,

Some men claimed they had lived on the bull's spittle, foaming in their ears and spilling in their mouths, salty as blood.

When the bull had whispered a long time, the boy came to know why he had never understood the talk of grass. The clans each spoke a different language, and the sounds blended into one. But now the boy heard each clan pleading with the bull, begging to prevail, begging to be spared by the long-toothed cows, begging the bull to strip the bark from all the trees that threatened with roots and shade the lives of the daughters of grass at the edge of the world, repeating again and again the annals of blades and clumps, rings and lines, chronicles of sisters, aunts and grandmothers, begging once again to be spared from teeth.

The music of a clan rose to a keening when the wives of a bull ate too many daughters. The bull lumbered from his resting place to butt his cows, nipping their flanks. He shook his horns and snorted. The wives moved on. The bull ambled back to his place. While there was salt in the boy's ears, the bull licked and whispered, whispered and licked.

In the long-ago days, cows carried their young for forty years. The calves learned to listen and talk inside their mothers; because they had not yet seen the world, they were impatient.

"Mother," they would say, "are your ears folded? My father tells you to move, so shake a hoof!"

The calves didn't know they would ever be born. They were fed through their stomachs and didn't use their mouths to eat. No wonder they talked so much.

They were born when their mothers grew tired of their scolding. They resisted, but still they slid, for their mothers had eaten mud to grease the birth slips. The calves opened their eyes to ripple on ripple of grass, the trees at the faraway edge of the grass dissolved in purple like the mountains behind them. The calves' knees shook and their legs wobbled. All those years they had scolded their mothers for eating grass, only to discover they must eat it themselves; "Now you are born," the mothers said.

The calves may have seen a boy lying between the great bull's hooves. They may have smelled the salt the bull was licking from the boy's ears and heard the murmur of the bull, whose words made no sense to the calves. Their father seemed to be telling the boy which calves to kill and eat! He told the boy he could take all the bull calves he liked, but no cow calves, though he could take old cows. If the boy broke these laws, the bull's anger would roll like thunder into the village, overturn the grain baskets, and tear up the houses. The bull would paw the earth from the graves; the dead accustomed to darkness would squint in the light, moaning as the bull gored their bones.

Then the bull would turn to the living, who would barely have time to hide their children beneath the overturned baskets. The bull would trample the fleeing men, and, with swinging horns, impale the women one by one; holding the napes of their necks between his teeth, he would mount them. Just before he snapped their necks like sapling twigs, they would each give birth to a monster with the feet and head of a bull, the body of a human. The monsters would beat on the village drums with their feet, eating the villagers' brushes of grass. Wild unspeakable songs would mount in the hearts of the children hidden under baskets. They would throw off the baskets, snorting like bulls and pawing the ground. Turning and turning they would dance to dizziness, then death. The monsters would eat their hearts, swollen with grief, and leave their flesh for the slinking dogs, then sniff the wind in all directions, smelling for other villages.

The boy who heard this knew what it meant to hunt. And if a calf who heard it was a bull, he knew he must not stay in the grass with his father and his father's wives. He must gallop to the far-off forest, up the far-off mountains, driving all the sisters before him he could. He must gallop until he no longer heard the echo of his father's murmuring in the ear of a boy; no longer heard his father's wives, munching while children complained in their bellies; no longer heard the clans of grass, pleading and mourning. The bull calf galloped to the forest, where trees battled their sisters for light. He galloped over the spines of the mountains, till he came to another world of grass which had no bull at its heart. This is what the young bull did, if he heard what his father said to the boy who lay between the hooves. But not all the young bulls heard.

When hunters entered the grass in search of meat, the grass parted to make a path, and the path always led to a bull calf. The hunters walked straight toward him, spears raised. They bellowed aloud the names of the women of their clans, first the living, then the dead. And the knees of the bull bent to the hunter who could sing the greatest number of names. He raised his spear to plunge it between the bull's shoulders, and he carried home meat.

But if anyone sang out the name of a male, the bull would charge. The hunter had to stand. If he turned or ran, there would be no meat; all the young bulls would flee. The old bull would move the cows, even the oldest, farther than a man can walk. The people would have nothing to eat but earth, for grass would sour in their mouths, the birds fly past their snares, nuts rot in the women's baskets.

If the hunter who had called the name of a male faced without flinching the rush of the bull, bore without wincing the horns puncturing his body, watched without blanching his blood rush into grass, and sang then correctly the song of descent through his mother's line, this bull, too, would bow his head. He would kneel. The hunter would plunge his spear between the shoulders of the bull, then die himself. Already in his village, the wind would be playing on the grass of the houses.

When a boy crawled from between the hooves, his salty ears licked clean, he knew what it meant to be brave. The grass parted to make a path;

the boy followed it, talking to the clans he passed, saying "Good morning" and "Good evening" in the language of each, though already his memories of grass talk were fading. Back in his village, his brothers ran to greet him, laying their drums in the grass for the wind to play. And although the boy was returning with only his cup, the drums played the meat song.

When white men came to the grasslands, we knelt before them. They believed we yielded to their strength, but we submitted because they had no more color than the wind that plays on drums. We thought they were our ancestors, risen from the mounds of bones beneath the earth. And the partings of their hair resembled the partings of the daughters of grass to make a path for our hunters.

Had we known they would dig up the grass, kill the bulls, kill the dogs and the bright-headed birds with their guns, we would not have bowed our heads. We would have given our wives to the bull, plunged our spears in our own breasts, spilled our blood in the grass. The monster children born to our wives would have eaten alive the wind-color men.

Now our boys have walked away. The daughters of grass—the long grass, the old grass—are barely remembered. Evenings the wind plays on dried-up drums the rhythms of songs from radios. The faithless wind and dry old women are all that are left. I eat rice from the white man's store. When I die, who will sing my mother's names? The world is not the same, no, the world will not be the same, HIIIIII. The world, I would say, is dead.

OONO

Ooni are the largest creatures on earth, huge blobs of flesh suspended on flippers. The North North ice creaks and groans beneath them. They slide into water gently as oil, and miles away the water rises; tidal waves and hurricanes crash in the tropics, all because an oono slid off the ice cap to fish.

Ooni cruise the depths opening and closing their mouths. They swallow schools of finger fish, whole seals, and even small whales. They only come up for air, rising to the top slowly, sometimes breaking ice with their heads. The cracks may resound for miles. A crack may even split the sky, making lightning flash. The ignook people hear the crack and see the flash. They say to each other, "The world lives."

Except for tusks that hang from the back of the upper jaw, an oono's mouth has no teeth. He opens and closes a sieve. Yet teeth guard the tunnel-like doors of the females' bodies. The males are afraid to enter the womb, so when a male smells a female in heat, he sends for a child who is already born.

"The doors of my wife have reddened," he says.

He drops his seed in a fold of his child's neck. The child flops across the ice to the mother, who has rolled on her back. The child climbs on her belly. He waddles to the birth door. He parts its lips with his nose and crawls past the teeth to the shelves where unborn children sleep. He places seeds on their tongues and crawls in beside them to nap.

Each tooth contains a spirit, a small, fierce, white spirit, like a mean dog. Long before the tongues of the children tasted the seeds of their fathers, the children's ears were licked by the dogs, whispering their secret names.

The dogs know when a young male has grown to maturity. He forgets the names of the dogs, and gives off a different smell. The grown male smells like burning whale fat; there clings to him no longer the smell of fur between the toes of a sleeping bear. Nor does the child smell cling to the grown female; she smells like the insides of fresh-killed fishes' heads. When the doors of her body are red, she smells like the marrow of caribou thigh bones. Her round eyes widen; her round nose twitches. Then the howl of her tooth dogs shivers the wind like the keening that follows the dead across the ice.

Before ooni had young, they could not mate at all. In those days there were but two ooni, a male named En-mai-mai and his wife En-mai-na-loo. They knew each other only by sight, for they lived far apart on the ice.

Sun had given En-mai-na-loo the tooth dogs. He told her En-mai-mai could only enter her body if she told him the names of the dogs. But this, said Sun, she must do, though she would weaken and wither, slow and die when her children were born. She could choose the time and place of En-mai-mai's entry, said Sun, but she could not refuse him entry. She could not choose to live forever because Sun would tire of seeing her sprawled on the ice. She must bear young, then die.

En-mai-na-loo wanted to live forever, so she vowed to trick Sun. She vowed she would never tell En-mai-mai how to get past the dogs. She sent her spirit across the ice to warn him: She didn't care how long her children slept inside her. To wake them was to fall toward sleep herself. The more children walked from her shelves, the less of her there would be. She had not yet gotten tired of being. En-mai-mai had, but he was afraid of the tooth dogs. They were not the death he had in mind. En-mai-mai would die by melting into snow, that he had decided, but meanwhile he would rest. Because En-mai-na-loo would not receive him, he rolled over on the ice. He turned his back. Then En-mai-na-loo rolled over. She turned her back. Without looking at each other, the ooni sprawled on the ice and slid off it to fish. The spirits of their hearts moved in and out of their bodies.

Heart spirits are not like tooth-dog spirits. They are mischievous and powerful but never mean. An oono's heart spirit is blue. It walks on water and sails on ice, naming and renaming different kinds of white, like *oo-ni-nak*, fresh-snowfall white, and *ni-ni-ya*, thin ice-over-water white. The spirit dives to the bottom of the sea and blows big bubbles to tip kayaks. It disappears by breathing out then reappears by breathing in. Sometimes it burrows deep into ice and hides while its huge body waits on top. Only when the spirit is hungry does it return to the stiff fat body. If oono heart spirits did not need their bodies to eat, they might never return to them—but that is another story.

Once an ignook trapped En-mai-mai's spirit and imprisoned it in his body. This ignook, the hunter Ain, grieved with his wife, Nuni, because their three children had all been born too soon. They had died before taking their first milk. Each time a child died, Nuni covered her face with her hair. And each time a child died, Ain took its tiny body to the place where the old and sick go to turn their backs. Each time he himself carved a death knife. He widened the path in the left nostril so the child's spirit could walk across the ice where the eyes of the dead burn through the night in their villages. Then he threw the knife in the sea to be a shark.

In those days the living did not build villages. There was not enough food, and the families of hunters lived far apart. That is why the wise older women could not get to Nuni in time to help with birth. The children died as Ain with his hunter's hands pulled them from her womb. Only the dead lived in villages then, the dead who do not have to eat. Even in the earliest days the dead had left their stomachs behind. All they had kept of their bodies was their eyes, burning like hearth fires; the napes of their necks, and their hair and nails, which keep on growing forever.

Even today, the dead weave their hairs together into houses without doors, with walls so tangled no one living, body or spirit, can penetrate. The dead can leave their houses at will but do not leave often. They pull hairs from the walls to make nests; they huddle in the nests telling secrets. They will not let the living hear them, but Nuni once tricked them. She had disguised her spirit as a gull and had flown over the edge of the world. She listened outside a dead house for words that would permit her to carry her children back to life—but that is another story.

When the spirit of a dead infant arrives at a hair-house village, the dead themselves mourn. For though they are happy in their nests, they remember how they loved to live before their bodies wore out. They remember the pleasure of yawning after eating, how sunlight could feel on the tops of their heads. They remember rubbing noses and scratching each other's backs. They remember the sound of water, humming under ice, the smells of food, the taste of tears. They tell the dead infant stories of what he missed in life. Because they no longer have any tears to let fall, they drop their finger- and toenails into the water, to sink to the bottom and turn into fish which have no eyes but see in the dark. These fish can swim right up to a death-knife shark and steal its food—but that is another story too.

When Ain returned from carrying his third child to the death place, his wife uncovered her face and cooked him a stew of seal fat and fish. She cried into the pot, and the stew was salty. Ain knew the salt taste was tears; he was loth to smack his lips at his wife's sorrow. He rubbed his nose against hers and she rubbed back. He knew she was keeping her grief to herself so she would not pain him. When she thought he slept she covered her face with the tent of her hair and wept some more. Ain did not open his eyes, for he wished to respect her sorrow, but cupped his hands around her hip bones. Ah, if ignook could live in villages, it would not be Ain's clumsy hands that pulled the babies from Nuni so forcefully he frightened them to death. Men were not meant to pull babies from their wives. Men were meant to get food. But how could Ain do this, when all the fish and even the seals hid beneath the closing ice the coldest hungriest parts of the year?

The body of En-mai-mai or En-mai-na-loo would have fed all the ignook for many winters, but it was impossible to kill an oono. Ain could not get close enough to throw the harpoon. The oono's breath was colder than the coldest wind, colder than ice itself. Ain would have frozen in its blast. Even a bear that walked far out on the ice was easier to hunt than Oono.

One stormy day Ain was sitting in his ice-block house carving fish, seals and bears on a walrus tusk. He was working on the shaft of a new harpoon; on it he was carving every animal he hunted. As he worked he chanted, "Oh, let my harpoon fly straight and true, straight and true, straight and true to the heart." The flame in the oil lamp flickered as he carved.

"Nuni," he said, "you mustn't make the air shake with careless breathing. When the air shakes, the light shakes; when the light shakes, my hand shakes. The harpoon I'm carving will waver on its course."

Nuni said she would breathe more carefully. She sat with her back to the lamp, but the flame still flickered.

"The wind is seeping through the chinks in our house," said Ain.

"I'll stop the chinks with spit," said Nuni, and she did, but still the lamp flickered.

Ain looked all around the house. What was shaking the light? What was shaking his hand? Skins and furs, spears and tools and sledge-dog harnesses—everything was as it always was. Then Ain noticed a blue light shining from the center of one of the ice blocks. He poked Nuni in the ribs.

"En-mai-mai's heart spirit has tunneled under the ice fields and up into our house," said Ain. "He's looking over my shoulder as I carve and making my hand shake."

"What has the spirit come for?" asked Nuni. "It must want something."

"I'll send my own heart spirit to talk," said Ain.

"Be careful," said Nuni. "My grandmother lost her self that way. She sent her spirit out disguised as a dog. When it returned she walked on four feet instead of two and snarled at her husband. She always took more than her share of meat and she howled with the dogs at the moon."

"I know what to do," said Ain. "I'm not so old my brains have turned to air."

He pasted a gull's feather on his forehead with wax from Nuni's right ear and rubbed his feet, hands and face with dried gull's blood. (Gulls shriek and chatter so; to this day Oono loathes the fuss they make.) Ain ate fourteen gull's eyes Nuni had preserved in walrus fat. Then he turned around, pulling on his left nostril and humming "NNNNNNNNNNNNNah-Nah, NNNNNNNNNN-Nah." His spirit flew from his left nostril.

Ain's body lay as dead, then, on the floor of the ice house. Nuni covered it with fur robes then crawled under the robes to keep the body warm. She blew breath into Ain's mouth and ears and kept her own ear to his chest, listening to silence where Ain's heart had beat: she was waiting, and she knew how.

Ain's spirit crept into the ice block where the oono spirit was hiding. There Ain saw Oono's spirit curled like a worm, muttering:

"First I was, then I was not. I formed like the ice from the sky. First there was black sky, then water sky, milk sky, then oono, spread over ice white as ice. The wind blows snow on our faces forever. I am tired. I do not want to be eaten by tooth dogs. I do not want to be eaten by ignook. But I do not want to live forever. I want to melt into snow.

"Seal and fish, rabbit and walrus, gull and bear—ooni are the only ones whose pictures ignook do not carve. We are the only ones who do not send children into the world. If I can talk this hunter into carving me on his harpoon shaft, my wife may permit a visit with seeds."

How could this be? Ain asked himself. En-mai-mai has never carried a baby to the death place; he grieves for young he has never had. Too bad he can't get close to his wife, but maybe all is well. At least they won't quarrel like my uncle Am-ni-noo-nau and his wife, Nan-nan, who pierced his heart with a fishbone as he slept.

In the center of the ice house, the lamp shuddered as the oono spirit sighed. Nuni hugged the cold body of Ain tighter. She opened the scar of the belly button and blew her breath inside the body.

"The hunter sleeps in his wife's arms, but soon he returns to his carving," said Oono. "I will watch him. Then I will make a picture of myself on a dart carved from my own tusk. I will smear the dart with my seed; I will shoot it into En-mai-na-loo's womb past the teeth. She will give birth to young. And I will melt into snow and die."

"You may be large and strong but you are dumb," said Ain's small yellow spirit to the oono's great blue one. "Shooting a dart into your wife will make children who are too injured to live. You'll have to leave them out on the ice with their noses cut off. Your heart will be so heavy you won't be able to swim or fish, and yes, you'll die, but yearning for your children. There will be no losing yourself in snow."

"OOOOarghgh," moaned the spirit of the oono. "What shall I do, Hunter? I know it is you; the gull stink does not fool me. I could kill your spirit by staring at it. Your wife would freeze by your still body as the lamp guttered. But I am not going to kill you. I have you at my mercy in the ice block where I know how to get out and you do not. You think you do, but you do not. The hole you made coming in has frozen shut behind you; you are too sleepy to make another one. I have you at my mercy, so I can ask any favor I want, and you have to grant it."

"Speak," said Ain's spirit, and showed the red spot on the nape of its neck.

"I am so large and my eyes so small I have never seen myself," said the oono. "Again I ask: On the dart you are carving, draw my body with those of the other animals."

"If this magic worked on a creature as large as you," said Ain, "we ignook would bury more meat than we could eat during all our lifetimes. I would be glad to draw your picture on the shaft of a dart, En-mai-mai, but I cannot take advantage of your stupidity. Besides, carving your picture would be hard.

"You're so large I can't see what you look like even when I can see your body. To understand its shape, I would need to make many journeys, long dangerous ones far into the ice fields. Only that way could I see the inlets and bays of your body. I would have to make drawings of your many parts on the backs of skins. Who knows how many drawings? How would I keep them straight? If you moved, as you would, while I was drawing, I would become confused. I would have to start over. I might spend my whole life figuring out what your body looked like, and still not get it right. Meanwhile, what would Nuni eat?"

"Yes, what would Nuni eat?" mumbled Nuni in her sleep. She had slept with first one of Ain's ears in her mouth, then the other. Sometimes his nose, sometimes one of his fingers or toes had been in her mouth. She did not want any part of his body to be cold when his spirit returned.

"Even if I learned how you look," said Ain, his spirit curling and uncurling in the center of the ice block, "how could I draw a body as large as yours on a dart shaft? It would be better to draw your body on the ice with the runner of my sledge. Your spirit self could sit on my shoulder to guide me. Better yet, I could draw your wife's body on the ice! Then you could hop from my shoulder into the womb of the ice wife, carrying your body's seed. Maybe young would be born."

"What about the tooth dogs?" asked the oono's spirit.

"I will draw no teeth," said Ain. "If no teeth, then no dogs."

Oono's spirit was so happy it put its feet in its mouth and rolled around inside the ice block. Ain's spirit had spoken truth, having shown the red spot on its neck, yet it had not told Oono all there was to tell; it felt heavy—not like rolling around with its feet in its mouth.

"My wife cannot keep my body warm too long," said Ain's spirit. "I must return."

The oono spirit too remembered its body and drilled a hole by turning its worm tail. The oono spirit crawled from the ice block through this hole and the human spirit followed. The blue light in the block went out.

A sudden dimming woke Nuni. She looked suspiciously at the lamp, but the wick was still glowing in the oil. Then Ain stirred in Nuni's arms. She rubbed his nose with her own and smelled the wind he exhaled. It smelled like seal mother's milk, as if he had slept in his body all night. Nuni was relieved and thumped her chest with the flat of her hand.

Even with Oono's spirit whistling guidance, drawing the oono's wife on the ice was hard. Ain first had to run the sledge far and fast to get up speed. He could not use sledge dogs, because the oono spirit thought they were tooth dogs. Besides, sledge dogs hear words that have not been spoken and repeat them in their sleep at night. Ain could not trust his dogs with the secrets he had kept from the oono. Sledge dogs lighten a hunter's load; they are company, but this was a pull across the ice Ain had to make by himself.

To get up speed without dogs Ain would have to run fast, breathing very deeply of very cold air; he feared he would freeze his throat or even his lungs. So before he ran the sledge out onto the ice, he heated his throat. He sat cross-legged on the ice just out of sight of his house and spoke to the sun as a friend. He told him about Nuni, how she laughed and showed the strong teeth she used to chew seal skins soft for clothes. He told about Nuni's legs, how she wrapped them around his body. And he told about the little pockets under her eyes, where she kept her tears, and about her breasts, which had at their tips all year long the little berries that grow where ice melts from patches of earth in summer, sweet short summer.

Hearing about Nuni the sun looked for her. When he saw her feeding sledge dogs near the house, he laughed and shone hot on Ain's throat. If Nuni had been lazy or ugly, if her teeth had been bad, her legs weak, the sun might have taken his warmth from Ain even as Ain was praising her. Ain would have died on the ice near his house. Nuni would have found him knotted stiff, with icicles under his nose.

As Ain traveled on his sledge, breathing deeply, he was glad to have Sun for a friend. He would rather have traveled by night, when the stars would have guided him over the ice, but he could not. The ignook traveling by night moves slowly, taking small, careful breaths of frozen air. He runs by the sledge to keep his feet from freezing; Ain was going to carve the body of the wife in one long coast, without lowering his feet from the sledge. So Ain was traveling far out onto the ice, where no living creature but the oono had gone before, and Ain was traveling by day. Long out of sight was his ice house. Long out of sight was Nuni. Ain was alone with En-mai-mai's spirit on his shoulder, and with a light sledge. If he did not carve the wife's body and find his way home quickly, he would starve.

Ain traveled far and fast, and the oono's spirit whistled on his shoulder. For strength Ain chanted the names of his ancestors. Then he chanted them again, and again. When he had not seen a bear for the time it took to chant the names of his ancestors three more times, he chanted stories. First he told how the ice came, then how the sun won his wife the moon from her father the sky. He chanted the story of how the bear tricked the seal into teaching him to fish, and he chanted the story of how the fish learned to swim in the shadows under the ice. When Ain had chanted all these stories, he was so far out on the ice, all he could see was white. Even the sky was white, though the sun was high in it. Sun looked sick, and Ain feared Sun would cough and make a storm.

Ain had run out onto the ice till he could run no more. Yet he had to carve the oono wife in one coast with only En-mai-mai's whistling to guide him. He could not coast, shove with his foot, then coast again. Ain had hoped the oono would relent, would allow him to push off with his foot now and then, but En-mai-mai had come to believe in the ice wife completely. The blue spirit claimed if the outline of the wife were not continuous, children would be born deformed.

Only a powerful hunter could have outlined the wife in just one push. But Ain was powerful. He had large lungs, a strong heart, and muscular legs. Nuni had rubbed his body with fish oil. She had sewn his trousers and parka tight as skin, with the fur facing in. As she had sewn she had sung, "O Wind, be my husband's friend. Ain is his name, a hunter and carver. I have made his clothes tight, so you will stream around his body like water around fish. You will not get lost in folds, Wind, not get lost in folds."

Nuni had slipped the fish-bone needle into the fur of Ain's parka just beneath his chin so he could sew his clothes if they tore.

As Ain veered and swerved to En-mai-mai's whistle, his runner cut a track which deepened to a chasm behind him. He carved the outline of the wife, then he carved a room inside her, turning tight to leave her body through the door he had carved going in. He leapt from his sledge and lifted it after him.

The sun was lower in the sky now—barely visible in thickening whiteness. Ain was wet with sweat; he was afraid he would freeze as it dried to an ice suit. Talking to the oono spirit, he moved his arms and legs slowly. He dared not push the hood of his parka off his face, though the top of his head was hot.

"You see how beautiful I've made your wife," said Ain. "Your flesh wife is not as beautiful as this one."

"This wife does not want me any more than En-mai-na-loo," said the oono's spirit. "Her doors have not reddened, and her tooth dogs do not snore."

Ain sighed. It was useless to point out once again he had drawn no teeth, no dogs.

"How did that fish get up here on the ice?" asked Ain, pointing away from the ice wife at nothing.

"What fish?"

"That white one way over there."

While the spirit of Oono was looking for the fish, Ain pricked his finger with the needle Nuni had stuck in his parka. He smeared blood from the hole in his finger on the doors of the ice wife's body. Then he put the needle in his finger to keep the hole open. He left the end of the needle sticking out like a tooth.

"I see no fish," said the spirit of Oono.

"Never mind," said Ain. "Maybe there was none. But look at my hand. I have stretched it into your wife's womb and she has bitten me. Now her teeth are stuck in my hand—you can see one poking from my finger. Hear the tooth dogs, howling like wind. And look at the wife—her doors are bright red."

"Noo-na-ha-oo, noo-na-ha-oo," sang the spirit of the oono. Whistling cheerfully, it entered the womb of the ice wife and looked for her unborn children sleeping on her shelves.

Ain was whispering to the dead, who can hear noises so soft no one else can hear them. Ain was calling the dead to come from their villages over the edge of the world:

"Old who died because you moved too slowly to follow the food and were left behind on the ice—children who died because your father could not kill enough to feed you—babies who died because women cannot live close enough to help each other with birth—come, now, all: Harden the walls of this womb so the oono's spirit cannot escape by tunneling through. Hover holding hands so the oono cannot float from the womb like smoke. Do not let him slip between your legs. I want to bargain with him. He will help us living find food. We will carry his seed to his wife, sending our sledge dogs before us to wag their tails at the tooth dogs. We will leave the oono's seed on the tongues of the not-yet-born."

The dead blew over the edge of the world and ringed the walls of the ice wife's womb. They were so cold the ice they were standing on hardened to rock. The oono's spirit could not tunnel through. The dead spread over the top of the womb a ceiling of fog so cold the oono's spirit froze upon touching it. The dead became the ice wife's womb, a bag of cold, a mat of hair, a wall of finger- and toenails sharper than teeth, pointing at the blush on the nape of the oono heart spirit's neck. So the spirit of En-mai-mai could not get out of the womb.

The oono then called on the sun for help: "Sun, you see how I have been tricked. This ignook has ice in the center of his heart to deceive me so. Shine a knife of light to cut it out."

En-mai-mai called on the sun in vain. Sun had turned his back. He was chewing a lump of fat as he walked across the edge of the world calling his wife, the moon. He wanted to enter her body. He wanted to make a silver blush spread on her fish-green skin. He paid no attention to the oono's heart spirit.

Ain said, "Now you're at my mercy, En-mai-mai, for only at a word from me will the dead break ranks to free you. It's my turn to speak, and yours to listen."

"So it is," said the spirit of the oono and showed Ain the red spot.

"En-mai-mai," said Ain, "If you would drive fish and seals from beneath the ice for us to catch, then we could live in villages. The wise older women could help the young wives give birth. The men would carry fewer babies to the death place."

"If ignook lived in villages," said En-mai-mai, "then sooner or later many hunters would band together to track the oono. Their wives would sew a huge bag to trap my breath. The hunters would put their ears to my body to listen to the current of my blood. They would follow it upstream to my heart. That is not how I wish to die."

"If you drive the fish and seals from beneath the ice," said Ain, "our bellies will always be full. We will have no hunger for your flesh. We will praise the oono who has given us food. We will never kill him."

"Why should I believe you?" the oono's spirit replied. "You have already tricked me into bringing my seed to this wife. Inside her womb are sleeping shelves of ice. I do not believe you will help me, but I do not want to stay here, ringed by the dead who do not smile. What choice have I but to promise what you ask?"

"It's true you've been led here through trickery," said Ain. "Yet I have not lied and I will not lie. And I will keep my promises."

"Then why not send your spirit out to show the blood spot on his neck?" asked Oono.

"In this cold place, even in the parka Nuni sewed, my body would die without my spirit," said Ain. "I will show the red spot on my spirit's neck if you will enter my body."

"How can I enter your body, Ignook? I am a male and you are a male."

"I have a special door," said Ain.

"I am not going through your left nostril," said Oono's spirit.

"The door is in my finger," said Ain.

The ignook extracted his wife's needle. A tiny bubble of blood glowed to mark the hole. When Ain saw the eyes of the spirit fasten on the bubble, he spoke the word *neegna* softly enough for the dead to hear. They dropped each other's hands. They floated up from the walls of the womb, wispy as breath, then vanished. Ain was holding out his finger to the spirit of the oono. The bead of blood gleamed like an eye. The oono's spirit sucked itself down to a worm and dove into the hole. Ain sewed it up, then put the needle back in the fur of his parka. He sang "La-ha-a-hoo-na nishi nishi nishi" so the spirit would not be able to drill a hole through his flesh to escape.

When the oono spirit heard the song, it realized it had been tricked. It flew around Ain's body screeching Eghhh! Eghhh! Eghhh! and pounded the walls of his chest, but Ain would not open the hole in his finger. Hoping to escape through Ain's left nostril—even to the black ice beyond the hair-house villages—the spirit tickled Ain's throat so he would sneeze, but Ain swallowed instead, and the spirit fell to the pit of his stomach.

At last the spirit tired of trying to escape. It curled around itself and sang "noo-na-ha-oo." It had never been in a human body before. It felt light as a fish. Its own body was so fat!

When Ain's small yellow spirit poked its head out from between two ribs, En-mai-mai's spirit thought of staring at it to kill it. But then it remembered that killing Ain's spirit would mean killing Ain's body. There would be no one to widen his left nostril, and the oono's spirit might rot in a rotting body. With a shrug the big blue spirit showed the red spot on its neck. The yellow spirit did the same. The two spirits called each other *brother* and agreed to share breathing. They curled around each other and sang "noo-na-ha-oo." They only looked up to make sure Ain's body was finding its way home across the ice.

With two heart spirits warming his body, and the stars for a guide, Ain pushed the sledge fast through the snow-tossed night. At his house, Nuni embraced him. Ain helped himself to the dried fish she spread before him.

"Thank you for your warmth, Spirit of En-mai-mai, " said Ain into the sleeve of his parka. "I could not have returned through the dark without it. Now I will let you out of my body."

"I do not want to leave," said the oono spirit. "I will ride with you. We will hunt seal or even bear on nights so cold your lungs would freeze without me. We will dive beneath the ice to catch fish. There will be plenty for ignook to eat. The ignook can settle in villages. And I will go with you into the womb of your wife. We will both leave seeds in the mouths of your children. They will pass to the world with two sets of wisdom."

Ain had been helping Nuni thread a needle. When the thread had passed through the eye and Nuni had knotted it, he opened his mouth to speak to the oono. He did not get a chance to utter a word, though, for Nuni's eyes grew large and her nose quivered.

"Your eye teeth are nearly as long as your chin," she shrieked. "You look like an oono."

"I have En-mai-mai's spirit in my body."

"No wonder you have eaten all the fish I dried to last the winter."

Ain sighed, for he was still very hungry. "I'm afraid that life will be as hard as before," he said. "En-mai-mai's spirit will help me hunt and fish but then eat most of the food. We'll still have to live far from others. We won't have as sight neighbor any older woman to pull the babies from your body. And yet the oono has promised, our children will live."

"There are many colors of snow," said the oono spirit inside Ain.

All night long Ain lay awake. Nuni threw her leg across him, but En-mai-mai's spirit whispered to Ain, "She has not painted her doorway red. It will not open, even if the tooth dogs sleep."

"Ignook need not wait for the doors to redden," said Ain. "Nuni has no tooth dogs; she's ready when she runs her finger up and down the crack in my buttocks, as she's doing now."

The oono's spirit would not be persuaded to enter Nuni's body, and Ain's spirit did not wish to be inhospitable to a guest. So Ain's spirit stayed with the visitor's, curling around it and sadly singing "noo-na-ha-oo, noo-na-ha-oo."

At first Nuni was puzzled. She pulled her hair across her eyes and peered at Ain from between the strands. Then she remembered the spirit of the oono was in her husband's body. She was not sure she wanted En-mai-mai's spirit to visit with her husband's. What huge creatures would grow on her sleeping shelves? She worried her belly would become so big she would no longer be able to sleep in the house by Ain. She did not want to sleep outside with the dogs.

"You smell like gull fart with the spirit of that huge lummox inside you," she said aloud to Ain.

En-mai-mai 's spirit heard her.

"I suppose you think you smell good," it said. "You smell like dead fish thawing and rotting."

These words came from Ain's mouth, Ain who had never spoken unkindly to Nuni.

Nuni's eyes were slits.

"Who would want a man who lets a stupid spirit like En-mai-mai's tell him what to do? I see I've not known you all these years."

"Who would want a wife whose words like the tooth dogs crush the spirit?" asked Ain.

"Yes," said En-mai-mai, "who would want a wife with no manners, who lies with her body too close to yours, breathing more than her share of air?"

"Not I," said Ain's spirit.

"Not I," said En-mai-mai's.

The two heart spirits curled around each other once again, singing "noo-na-ha-oo." Ain's body rolled so his back was to his wife.

"We'll see about this," said Nuni. She pricked her finger with a needle. She smeared the doors of her body with blood. She lay very still in the dark with her legs apart while her spirit, her little yellow spirit, sat cross-legged on her forehead and sang:

"Hundreds of colors of dark in the cave of birth. Who knows their names? Not the unborn, whose eyes are closed, who cannot open their fists. In skins of dark on shelves of dark, they curl with knees to mouths, dark at the roots of their hair, dark between their toes, dark behind their ears and beneath their tongues. Who will seed with light their tongues? Who will name the colors of dark and make the children see?"

Then the two male spirits, proud of their knowledge, walked through the doors to Nuni's body. They lay seeds on the tongue of an unborn child, the first they found. The unborn smiled and wiggled his fingers and toes. Twenty-three months later Nuni gave birth to a son named An-muq who did not die when Ain pulled him out of her womb.

An-muq had two heart spirits, a blue one and a yellow one. He could carve and swim and talk as soon as he was born. His first words to his parents were, "Let's slip under the ice to fish." He needed no sledge but slid across the ice on his belly, jiggling his feet to steer. A great hunter even as an infant, he was desired by women despite his fat white body and long, tusklike eyeteeth. He would not marry. However, he would send his spirits disguised as two white dogs, a large and a small one, to join the sledge dogs when ignook wives were feeding them. The little dog would crawl up a wife's trouser leg. When she went in her house and took off her trousers to see what was lumping the leg, the big dog would follow the little one into her womb. In this way, many more fat, white children with long eyeteeth were born among the ignook than two-spirited Ain could father with Nuni.

As An-muq grew older, he spent more and more time by himself in his house carving pictures of animals on the snaggle-toothed combs that tangle the hair of dying ignook so their houses across the ice will have walls no sound can escape. The spirits of the animals he carved visited him and told him what they saw beneath their eyelids when they slept. They told him of the time long before when the spirits of dead animals lived in villages with the spirits of dead people. This was before people had tasted meat. Nor did animals eat each other in those days. Every creature ate ice. So An-muq claimed the animals had told him. Who knows whether it is true?

No one but his mother paid much attention to An-muq muttering alone in his house. Nuni touched his toes and stroked his ears. "Dear boy," she said, though An-muq's hair was only less gray than her own. "We did not make the world." An-muq touched his mother's wrists. He asked her to keep his body warm while he sent his spirits across the ice, disguised as two white dogs. He sent them to the body of En-mai-na-loo, who still lived and breathed on the ice. The white dogs regurgitated meat near the doors of her womb. Her tooth dogs rushed to get the meat. An-muq's spirits nipped into the womb. This was the first time a child of En-mai-mai carried his seed to his wife.

Twenty-three months later En-mai-na-loo gave birth to twelve daughters and twelve sons, each with two heart spirits. They looked like ooni, though with round ignook noses and round ignook eyes. En-mai-na-loo howled when she saw them, but she let them drink from her nipples. The blue and yellow spirits of An-muq watched the children till the ice broke beneath their weight and they sank into the water to fish. Then the spirits returned to An-muq's house, where Nuni had been blowing breath into his nostrils. Although his body was warm throughout, he was weak and could hardly eat. He lay with his head on his mother's lap sipping fish broth. When he tried to talk he barked, but his parents knew. An-muq no longer wanted to live, so Ain widened his son's left nostril. The yellow spirit of An-muq went to the villages of ignook dead. The blue one went to the black ice where the oono dead live far apart.

Ain fished and carved long after An-muq had died, but finally his time came. He walked to the death place and stuck his knife up his left nostril. His oono spirit returned to En-mai-mai's body, which had been sleeping on the ice all along; the big blue heart spirit lived another long life there. Then, the time having come for En-mai-mai to die, he leaned on one of his tusks till it broke. He rubbed his nose against it to widen his left nostril. His body melted at once into snow.

When En-mai-na-loo died, the sun came for her. He called the tooth dogs by name and stabbed the heart of each with an icicle of light. Lifting in his arms En-mai-na-loo's enormous body with the heart spirit still inside, he carried her way beyond the black ice to hide her in a cave in the darker-than-dark. When the body of his moon wife dwindles, he visits En-mai-na-loo's cave. Some say En-mai-na-loo grows stars on her sleeping shelves, even though she is dead, but how could that be?

To this day, no ignook will harm an oono; no oono will injure an ignook. The ooni have round noses and eyes. The ignook have long eyeteeth. These are pulled from the mouths of the dead before the bodies are taken out on the ice. Hunters carve weapons from the ivory of the teeth. It is also carved into finger rings which no one will wear, though many ignook carry them in pouches around their necks. They claim words issue from the pouch mouths: *La-ha-a-hoo-na nishi nishi nishi; neegna, neegna;* and *noo-na-ha-oo.* Like the hope of the dead for the living, these words spread around the ignook, to keep them warm if they are stranded far and alone on the ice at night.

BLACK FOOD

A long time ago and very far away it was never as I will tell you. What didn't happen, did, and what did happen didn't. Yet then as now, a man who paced in the dark in a cave, muttering and murmuring all summer, a man who ignored the game in the season of pursuit, such a one might starve when the dream-time fell on us cold and white from the sky. Come winter, provident hunters gave themselves at last to their visions, living on what they had stored. He who had dreamed in summer must now track beasts through snow, praying to find a bear that had entered his cave late and thus left prints atop the white-fall.

Long ago, there lived such a man, a summer dreamer named Talks to Himself. Talks to Himself had a woman, a round, bright one named Sun Daughter who still wore her deerskin wedding dress, for they had not been married long. Sun Daughter shook her head when she saw Talks to Himself pacing day after day in his cave, murmuring and muttering the summer away while other men brought in game. She walked more and more slowly, with her head hung low, but she spent her days gathering fat-roots and drying sweet-berries, lest she and her husband starve when the cold time came. One day she followed a berry-gobbling bear into the woods. "His Hugeness knows where the best bushes are," she said. "I'll follow where he can't see me picking what he leaves behind." And so she skulked along in the shadow of the huge one. And she disappeared. She was not seen around the cooking fires or in the houses of stretched skin for a very long time.

Talks to Himself looked all over for his wife, behind trees, even under rocks, but he couldn't find her, only a scrap of deerskin impaled on a thorn, fluttering in the wind. Talks to Himself plucked the scrap from the thorn, and he put it into his ear, where it would be safe, though he could not hear himself talking very well. You could say that was a good thing. The days were getting shorter. Talks to Himself had very little food for winter, only what Sun Daughter had left, which was already running out.

Men had scant pity for Talks to Himself, for he had brought his trouble on himself, so he padded around the women, begging. The women fed him because they liked his talking—story-talk, they called it—though now he only chewed his fingernails and told no stories. Alas, no matter how many dried berries those women flung at Talks to Himself, he found neither Sun Daughter nor any game, and none of his stories came back to him. Even when he sat in the cave for hours as his breath clouded around his face, no story came to tie up the world, and he felt it falling apart. Soon his skin hung in folds from his bones. His eyes grew dull, and the old ones in his village nodded to each other.

"He will starve," they said. "And not for lack of food, for our women throw him enough to keep him alive."

They saw he would perish if he stayed by the fires, so no one tried to stop him when he walked out into mist and snow, barefoot and naked but for his loincloth.

There would be nothing more to tell if he hadn't eventually returned. Nonetheless, Talks to Himself disappeared into the snow cloud beyond our fires and walked through it just above the earth, his feet not touching the ground. When he had walked a long time, he thought he saw the gray fires of the dead smoldering along the horizon. He wasn't looking where he was going, so he stumbled on a pile of stones and fell into a cave—not his story cave, another one. At first he didn't even know he was in a cave. All he knew was the crash and clatter of his landing. Feeling with his hands, though, he touched a wet, cold ceiling just above his head. For a while he saw only darkness, then he saw some people who were nothing but bone and ghost—dead people who had not yet agreed to let go of earth—who were loitering around waiting for something to happen.

Talks to Himself said, "All summer long my talking fed me, but now stories and dreams have fled. I might as well be dead, so here I am."

The bone people said, "You can't stay here with us. Your flesh is still strong and salty. Your body needs food now; we eat only the odor of food."

Talks to Himself said, "Please, I only want to look around. Maybe there is a woman here who can cook for me. Maybe my woman is here."

The bone people said, "You can't stay here."

"How will I find my woman then? I've looked all around everywhere up there."

The bone people said, "Call Crow. He likes to find things. He smells everything. Maybe he'll carry you through the snow cloud to where your woman is."

The bone people asked if Talks to Himself had anything Sun Daughter had worn, a dress or a shoe, anything with her scent still ripe in it.

"She walked away in her clothes," he said. "There's only a tiny scrap from her skirt that snagged on a bramble when she stumbled into the forest after the huge one."

The bone people said, "That's enough. Climb out of our house. Make a crow-call as best you can. Crows aren't fussy. Give Crow the scrap, then stand away, or your smell will distract him. Before you go, rub your greasy armpits over the cairn you'll see above our house. We bone people can live a long time on a whiff of stink like yours."

Talks to Himself did just what the bone people said to do. He took the scrap of his wife's dress out of his ear. He made a crow-call the best he could. And he threw in a few secret words he happened to know. He gave Crow the scrap of his wife's dress, and he stood well away, as he had been told to do. The crow shook his head.

"You smell too strong," he said. "Too human. I can spare two nice sleek, black feathers from my tail. Wash your body in the river there where the ice doesn't cover the water. Dry yourself by rubbing on tree bark. That way you'll leave some musk for the bone people when they come out of their cave next spring. Hold my feathers between your fingers. If you're lucky and don't sweat, you may pass for a crow. Then you can follow me anywhere and talk to anyone."

They began flying all around then, flying in circles, so it seemed to Talks to Himself. But after a while the crow saw something down on the ground. "Look at that," he said, but the man saw nothing, only the snow cloud they were inside. He kept looking, though, looking where Crow was looking with his sharp little eye. After a while the man saw Sun Daughter. She was running in the snow but getting nowhere. He knew it was she. He could tell from the sound of the shells on her dress jingling as she moved. It was Sun Daughter all right, in her deerskin wedding dress, the dress she had made herself, the only one she had. She was running around in the snow, carrying an empty basket and sobbing.

"You hover up here," said Crow. "Just fly in circles. It's easy. You lower one wing and raise the other, flapping all the while. That's it. . . . I'm going down there to do what I can."

Crow descended to earth and stood a little way off from Sun Daughter with his head cocked. He was looking with his sharp little eye at the woman's empty basket, listening to the snow-fall. He listened a long time, and then he shook his head so hard in disbelief his feathers fell off his body. He was just a poor plucked meat-thing then, shivering in the cold. Sun Daughter was weeping with her hands over her eyes. She didn't notice Crow shivering beside her in the snow. How could she help him? She couldn't even help herself. Crow would freeze if Talks to Himself didn't fly down there. He trembled to think his wife would see he had come after her and run away again, but Crow had been good to Talks to Himself, who couldn't just let him freeze. So Talks to Himself flew down to Crow and began picking up the feathers that were blowing around in the wind, hopping and grabbing and sticking the feathers back on Crow's body where they belonged. And pretty soon Crow's body was covered again. Some of his feathers were lost forever, but most were saved. The crow and the man each called out their relief and joy, the crow with a CAW, the man with a man-sound, a yipping whoop.

When Sun Daughter heard the man-sound, she stopped running. She stood very still and she stared at the man and the crow, a puzzled look on her face.

"She doesn't know me any more," said Talks to Himself.

"You're carrying two of my tail feathers between your fingers. She thinks you're a crow," said Crow. "She knew your voice, but she thinks it's the voice of a ghost."

"My poor woman! I'd better give you back these feathers and go to ease her mind."

"Not so fast," said Crow. "Maybe you had better hear her story first. Then you'll know whose woman she is now."

"How can I hear her story if she won't talk to me?"

"I could tell you the story," said Crow, "but it would be better if you heard it from her. It's so sad, you will have to keep your distance. Go back in those trees there, climb into one, and call down in Crow these words I am about to tell you. Say, 'Telling a story means jumping into the heart of it, then you go on from there.' See if she starts talking."

"I can't remember what I was doing before," said Sun Daughter. "I remember smelling His Hugeness, the honey-paw, and smelling the berries hot and ripe in the sun. Then I remember following His Hugeness further and further into the forest. Every time I thought I would never see the sun again, so dense and thick had the trees become, we would enter a clearing where sunlight made everything bright and lovely, and berry bushes again grew thick and fragrant and tall. No matter how many berries Honey-Paw swiped from the bushes with his claws, there were always berries left for me. I filled my basket. When I got hungry I ate, and filled my basket again. In this way I walked further and further into the forest, growing fatter and fatter, never noticing how the sun was falling asleep in the sky, which was growing darker as the air grew colder and the leaves began to flutter from the trees. At last I could see nothing at all on the trail ahead of me, but only followed the smell of His Hugeness, walking on four feet now. It grew colder and colder and soon snow fell through the bare branches of the trees, covering the tracks of the huge one.

"Drawn on by his scent I followed him still further, and soon we were walking down a tunnel burrow far into the earth, the smell of the soil warm and moist around the huge one's smell. Then we were in a small room far beneath the earth. And Honey-Paw turned his back to the room's door and shat a huge plug of scat that shut up the room. Then he slowly removed his suit of glossy black fur, and folded it carefully, and sat down naked and looked at me. Even in the dark, I could see he was a handsome young man, with bright, glowing eyes, shiny teeth, and lustrous skin. He was smooth to the touch, and soft. I liked him, and I lay with him, and then I fell asleep.

"When I woke up, a baby was crawling from between my legs, a shapeless lump of flesh with feet and hands. Honey-Paw was putting his bear clothes back on, and now he was furry again. His smell was stronger than ever, a smell of meat and fermented berries. My squirming, shapeless baby howled in my ear and hurt me. I threw him from me. The big furry one picked him up and licked him and licked him, snuffling and grunting, until he had licked him into the shape of a boy. Then he licked his own paw until his mouth was full of—yes, honey—honey and milk and fur. He made that fur into a suit for the bare red boy, smoothing it over him carefully. The boy wanted to drink my milk then and nuzzled me and nuzzled me. I let him suckle my breasts, which flowed with milk that smelled of honey and meat. His Hugeness bathed his paws in the milk that dripped from our suckling youngster's mouth and licked his paws to nourish himself, then he began clawing at the door plug until it gave way. With barely a glance behind him, he lumbered into a world that was bright, not with the first fresh light of spring, but with the soft reflected radiance of snow, for winter was still swirling and drifting over everything. The huge one told me to stay with our child while he went to wake up the world.

"Alas, I yearned to curl into the bear's gaminess and to lick his honeyed, meaty paw. Leaving my boy asleep in his warm, dark suit of fur, I put on my deerskin dress. I followed Honey-Paw out into the cold, but he ran away from me, as if he didn't know me, further and further into snow. I had no suit of fur. I grew colder and colder. After awhile I wanted to return to my child in our house beneath the earth, so I could suckle him. But the falling snow had covered the tracks. I could no longer see the way to the door of Honey-Paw's house. And more and more snow was drifting around me. *Aieeeeee! How can I return to my child, who will die without my milk?*"

"She is Honey-Paw's woman now," murmured Crow. "She doesn't know you."

"This may be true," said Talks to Himself. "But I promised her parents and her uncles and aunts and all the elders of our village I would cherish this girl. I can't leave her in the cold. She ran away from me; the honey-pawed huge one ran away from her. And now she grieves for her child, whom she left in the cave to starve. See how she weeps and walks in a circle! We must help her find her child. Then she can decide which of her husbands she will lie with. I say this. But I do not know how to find the cave if the snow has covered the tracks of woman and great furry honey-paw."

"You forget who I am," said Crow. "I can see backwards and forward in time. I can see the tracks of the woman and the honey-paw beneath the snow, before it fell. I will fly above and call out the way to you below. You must take my feathers from between your fingers—give them to me for my tail; without all my tail feathers, I struggle to fly straight—and walk like a man to clear the way for the woman through the snow."

Crow flew backwards, calling out the way, and soon they had found the place of the cave, its doorway under the roots of a tree covered with drifted snow. Crow brushed off that heavy blanket of snow with one sweeping flap of his wings. The hole was plugged up, though they could hear a loud sucking sound from within. "The huge one is feeding his son," said Crow. "The boy licks his father's paw and suckles himself on honey and fat."

"That is Honey-Paw's own winter food," said the woman. "He will dwindle in his skin as he sleeps while his son grows large and fat."

"And what of us?" said the man. "We are cold and hungry here in the snow. We cannot survive by licking our hands."

"I will call to His Hugeness," said the woman.

She put her mouth to a tiny crack at the edge of the plug in the door to the cave. "O great huge furry honey-paw!" she cried. "My tongue is hungry for the cracks between your toes."

No sound but the mournful, hungry sighing of wind.

"Will you leave the mother of your son to starve in the snow?"

Still no reply but from wind, blowing harder now.

The man and the woman and the crow could hear the rattling of their own bones as wind clawed at their skinny bodies.

"Aieeeeeeeeeee," cried the woman, scratching her cheeks with her nails. "We are bone people waiting at this scat-plugged door." She beat her fists against it to no avail.

"Talk," said Crow to the man. "Talk the stories that sustained you all summer while others were hunting game."

"Those stories never worked," said the man. "Sun Daughter left me for the huge one."

"Each thing in season," said Crow. "Maybe your stories are strong enough now." So the man talked story. And sure enough, the plug crumbled. Maybe someone was pushing it from behind, too.

It crumbled to bits around a tall young man who was emerging from the cave, naked, his hair long around his shoulders, his eyes bright and his smile radiant.

"My husband," cried the woman. "Do you stand in the snow without your suit of fur?"

"Mother, it is I," said the tall, naked young man. "My father has given me his strength and has died in my arms in our cave. He asks that we carry his body to the houses of stretched skin to feed those who have been looking in the trackless white for game. You and Talks to Himself may cut off his ears and his paws to nourish yourselves. The rest of the meat you must fairly divide, not forgetting the portions due the four directions, the sky, the earth, and that power which is under, above, and around all that we know. Wind must be remembered; thunder, lightning, rain; the oceans and lakes, rivers and streams; the trees; the creatures large and small that are eaten in season, and every useful and beautiful plant. Give thanks and a portion of the meat to all that lives and all that has died, though the smoke from cooking meat and the smell of dripping fat will be enough for the bone people. If you do these things, all will be well. My father will give himself to the children of my children and to their children's children. There will be black food when snow whitens the ground."

Talks to Himself and Sun Daughter packed the meat out of the cave. The son of Honey-Paw returned with them to the village, though he would not bend his back to the burden of his father's flesh. The village feasted; winter was long that year, but no one starved. Even the oldest and the youngest could be fed. Before he walked back into the forest on two feet then four, the son of the huge one taught us how to hunt in winter, how to divide the meat, and how to live a grateful life. When he had eaten, with Sun Daughter by his side, Talks to Himself talked story after story, and everyone learned the stories by heart. And Crow? He was happy to peck at scraps around the cooking fires. Later, when grain was harvested, he was content to be given a portion of the gleanings. He did not ask for more, for he did not wish to upset the order of the world, the way its hungers balance.

AFTERWORD

In *The Hungry Girls* Patricia Eakins writes of terrifying pullulation with enormous charm. Nature—Mother Nature—appears gargantuan and omnivorous, a composite of Kali and Persephone ascendant and vengeful. The stories certainly trash the Romantic Landscape; the cornball one, that is, not the one that has always been out there, darwinian, epiphanaic, rife with metamorphoses. Readers who have witnessed something like a gypsy-moth caterpillar onslaught, the denuded summer woodland, or who have been just as surprised to see nature rebound with awesome abundance will recognize the effect. Such abundance and devastation, powerful, fierce, and weird, become in Eakins's imaginative stories not a setting but a force, conveying Wordsworth's often neglected message that nature "teaches" as much through her fearsomeness as her sublimity.

Stories patly based on a single effect do not adequately capture a sense of significant experience. The momentous is never purely one effect but an awesome mix of feelings, often contradictory, that overwhelms one simultaneously. We're surprised to find, speechless as we are, that we can contain them all. Isn't that what the good writing does?

One never gets the feeling, as in some bestiaries, that the author of *The Hungry Girls* is a person-of-letters and the stories are an amusement. The many humorous notes Eakins hits do not lighten her stories' seriousness but accentuate it, perhaps because, in a world in which life is an omnivorous blind force, the blessings and rewards are bound to be accidental and ironic, e.g., the beauty of life is redeeming; in this she reverses Rilke, as if to say that beauty is not the beginning of terror but survives it.

Eakins has a Rabelasian ability to make anything, even geophagy, fascinating. A calm, superior, matter-of-fact tone gives her prose an unnerving edge, yet the sentences of, say, "Snakeskins," are playfully, effectively rhythmic; the contrast of subtle, bemused, distanced narrator describing momentous events is a wonderful effect, as is the sense of deep rapids when the speed of the narration belies the depth of the story.

"Snakeskins" is powerfully and convincingly imagined, a sympathetic satire, a fabulist's explication of religious psychology and the longing for immortality. Its imagery is as poetic as that in, say, "Salt," which presents a stunning photography of decay, violent destruction and regeneration, mayhem in the matrix, or that in "Oono," though the visual beauty of the latter is more cinematic, more cinescopic—a matter of scale. "Oono" reads as if a documentary camera aimed at some Bering-Strait folk had focused on their collective unconscious and followed their beliefs into the cosmological realm: gentle grotesquerie and strangely gentle violence in a landscape realized as ethereal images, half-abstract to begin with, through which loss of innocence is traced—there are a great many aspects to all these stories; their spiritual range is that of an encompassing vision.

The stories constantly draw the reader in to view, in carefully defined close-up most of the time, life in a constant turmoil of metamorphoses, a Heraclitian but marvelous strife. So many of her creatures, in their very genesis, even in their prenatal state are already causing havoc, seething beneath the soil of edenic landscapes, bursting forth to reduce human affairs to defenseless absurdity. This is perhaps too general a comment; her stories are more complex and rich than any such comment can encompass, but the observation is applicable, even so, to "Salt," "Yiqh-Yaqh," "Snakeskins," "The Hungry Girls," "The Change," "Banda," "Farrago," "Murumoren," "Auravir"—mellifluous titles, many of them one-word poems that one can imagine Poe gloating over. Not such an idle remark that, since much of the tension in the stories derives from loving descriptions, painstaking details, of the wildly horrendous creatures. One might suspect that she had worked in a bio lab, for she describes with professional exactitude, an exploratory gaze, studious and passionate at once. Heraclitus: Nature loves to hide; Eakins: and to seek.

For all their careful observation, the stories in this modern bestiary have the furious motions of myth as an undercurrent. Perhaps their main focus is on the Imagination reclaiming its territory from Science, but the myths span the entire cosmological-biological range of creation and destruction. They sometimes read like re-enactments of ancient myths applied to familiar genres: the western, the feral child, the nuke mutant, the courtly Japanese tale, the Persian parable. . . .

So much of what Eakins is doing is reminiscent of the best of contemporary poetry—playing parodic homages off the conventions yet making them her own, for one: the way the stories move, for another: narratives that rely not so much on "plot" as on more realistic progression, cumulative and revelatory, the tension sustained by the brilliant description, the growth and effects unfolding as the author eyes them. Or, when the narrative is swifter, per demands of the genre, the "historical" or "adventure" tales, there is no formula ending but a scandent lyricism, as in "Salt."

I know that I am reading something wonderful when it renders the usual analytical tools obsolete. Patricia Eakins's work has the multifarious appeal of genius, and she may have written a major book. Certainly she has written a magical one.

—*Paul Violi*

A CONVERSATION
WITH PATRICIA EAKINS

Françoise Palleau-Papin

Françoise Palleau-Papin is professor of American Literature at the University of Paris 13-Sorbonne Paris Cité. This conversation took place on June 4, 1998, on a balcony overlooking the river in the village of Montolieu, near Carcassonne. Eakins was staying at the International Inkwell, a wonderful pension for writers in Montolieu, which is the French book-village in the Languedoc.

The conversation began with comments on Patricia Eakins's collection of stories, *The Hungry Girls and Other Stories*. I wanted to know from her whether "Daddy's Ibbit Wife" was about Vietnam, and its last paragraph about draft dodgers—"the dead who didn't get to Canada . . . the dead who didn't make it." I asked her whether I was completely imagining things.

Patricia Eakins: You are! But you were right to think of war, and flight from war. A more appropriate historical reference than the flight of Vietnam draft dodgers would be the forced migrations of Native Americans during the nineteenth century—the "Trail of Tears," the forced march of the Cherokee from Georgia to Oklahoma. Or the fighting retreat of the Joseph band of the Nez Perce, who were pursued by the bluecoats from Oregon through Idaho and Montana to the Bear Paw Mountains just south of the Canadian border. They had been heading for sanctuary in Canada as, in "Daddy's Ibbit Wife," the dead were. My story is not about the Nez Perce or the Cherokee or the Pueblo, however. It's about a made-up group of people.

Françoise Palleau-Papin: That clarifies it. What about the quote that was made up in the epigraph—"I give you here the flora and fauna of all the continents, beasts and vegetables, birds and fish, I have seen myself and heard reported. Mind there are many wonders under the sun. Which are God's creations? Which are men's? The truth is not always the likeliest story; thus I credit any careful account. Jean Louis Le Montal, in the foreword of his *Encyclopedia*." There is no Jean Louis Le Montal?

PE: No. And also, the names of the French towns are made up, of course.

FP: I didn't even check that out. Why would you make that up, and not clarify the fact that it's made up?

PE: Just to mystify. . . . [laughter]

FP: Just to mystify readers?

PE: Well, it's naughtiness, it's tongue-in-cheek, it's my sense of humor. If no one knows it's made up you might wonder what's funny, but it just struck me as entertaining to do it.

FP: It is entertaining, but also, it doesn't sound made-up at all, it sounds genuine in the way you put it—

PE: Le Montal said what I—you know, he's one more mask. I mean he speaks for me; he gives a voice to my aesthetic: "The truth is not always the likeliest story"—this is a very different aesthetic from the prevailing one.

FP: You mean that the prevailing aesthetic would be that you have to tell the truth, and nothing but the truth?

PE: Right. The prevailing aesthetic would be the memoir mentality—that a story should be the truth—

FP: A testimony?

PE: Yes. It's a truer story if it's confessional, if it has a non-fiction base, a confessional or factual truth. I kept reading about how science in the past hadn't been careful to distinguish between fact and fancy. And I began to wonder—perhaps science had taken a route that took it away from poetic truth.

FP: Yes.

PE: The older way of going about it, which was much more ingenuous, expressed truth of a different sort.

FP: Poetic truth that would be closer to the "real" truth?

PE: Well, it's another kind of truth. Actually, there was a French natural historian named Buffon—you probably know him. I read somewhere that he was the last great scientist who, given a choice between the most precise way of saying a thing and the most vivid, chose the vivid. I couldn't find a quote from him that said what I wanted to say, so I made up Le Montal. If I had found one of Buffon, I might have cited him, because I like him very much. It was a hugely important moment in human history when people describing the natural world began to choose the precise words and called that the truth and shied away from the vivid. People stopped wanting—now people don't even want fiction in their fiction.

FP: They're afraid of it.

PE: Yes, there's a certain suspicion—if it's invented it can't be true—

FP: It's fantasy. . . .

PE: Right, "mere" fantasy.

FP: I had a question in this respect, concerning your essay "Manifesto of a Dead Daughter[1]."

PE: That is a memoir.

FP: Right, but in it you also seem to be talking about different truths. You said: "the episodes of my opera radiate an antique melodrama that is hardly of this century"—and then you go on to say "Yet the arias were real, the snipers were real."

---

1. *Race Traitor: The Journal if the New Abolitionism*, ed. John Garvey, Noel Ignatiev. No. 4. Cambridge, MA. New Abolitionists, Inc. (Winter 1995): 1–5.

PE: Right.

FP: This is vivid.

PE: Well, "Manifesto" is a different kind of writing, you know. Here when I say real, I mean verifiable.

FP: This is a different kind of writing. Yet don't you incorporate biographical material, although disguised, in your fiction?

PE: Oh, sure. As I wrote "The Hungry Girls" I very consciously had in mind my husband's sister's two-year-old son Niko, who was truly a force of nature, loud, active, willful and destructive. Deep down I admired him enormously.

Niko was a source of inspiration for "The Hungry Girls," and his father Quentin, a rural veterinarian, is in it too. Around the time I wrote the story, I had had my appendix out. At the time, I was very thin. Quentin asked if the surgeon had given me a discount. Then he paused and thought quite a while. He asked, "Can you imagine what it is like to operate on a fat beagle?" This little conversation echoes the world of Rabelais, where the boundaries between *human* and *animal*, between *brain* and *body*, seem to have been more permeable than they are in the world that I live in, the urban world where people sit at computers all day long then go to the gym to work out on more machines.

Niko and Quentin live on a farm, among horses and goats and sheep and other animals, whose bodily needs and ways assert themselves along with those of humans. The farm world has such a rich smell of animals, their unbathed bodies and their excrement. Sometimes, when I sniff the powerful odor of a homeless person on the subway, I realize that everyone at a medieval/renaissance carnival or in an Elizabethan theater probably smelled quite a bit like this. Throw in the oranges and the pomanders and the bear garden not far off and some open sewers—and you begin to realize that, by contrast, we already live in the shadowy world of the television tube or the computer screen. The thin, cerebral, utopian future is already here.

FP: So "The Hungry Girls" is the only story in the collection that incorporates disguised biographical material?

PE: Well, maybe "transformed" is a better word than disguised. My life is always in there somehow. Even stories that I didn't think were very—for instance when you asked me about the draft dodgers—I began thinking about "Daddy's Ibbit Wife." For all that is invented, this is still the world my father was born in. He was not a Native American, but his ancestors did go out West in a covered wagon. I have a branding iron with—I don't think it's Bar-B, but a brand that was used on cattle belonging to my father's father. My father was born in a sod house, and there is this sense of going underground in "Daddy's Ibbit Wife," burrowing into the earth, into a sod realm. It's an echo of my family's story.

FP: Becoming an animal in a burrow. . . .

PE: Well, my grandmother ran away from my grandfather's ranch to become a Christian Scientist in San Francisco. I was always told that life on the ranch was "too animal" for her—too much birth and death. The crumbled burrows and grass-grown mounds of the story are an echo of the cornfield that I was told had been my father's birthplace. And then—you know, there is a playful aspect to my animal invention that is common to most of the stories in *The Hungry Girls*. It amused me to take real animals and give their characteristics to people—the reverse of fables. I coined this phrase "counterfable." I don't think it's sufficient . . . for one thing, my animals tend to be invented, though they are like real animals. The ibbits have a lot of woodchuck or prairie dog in them. As for why the counterfable project, I just think it's how I see the world—I really don't see people as being separate from animals, to the extent that you could say "animals and people." I think it would be closer to the truth to say "people and other animals." Why I had to explore that idea in such a lot of different ways is hard for me to say, though I have often been asked. It just appealed to me to do it.

FP: Yes. The way you work with it is very vivid. Talking about animals, your animals are very often, in your words, "vermin," like rats (I'm talking about "The Garden of Fishes" here[2]), and I was wondering—you say that the master does not record vermin in his book, he does not draw them—I was wondering to what extent you were trying to give a voice to what's been left out of . . .

---

2. *The Paris Review* 140 (Fall 1996): 202–212.

PE: Oh, I think so—

FP: . . . out of what you call "his chaste pencil and chalks," that is, vermin and slaves (I'm bringing them together on purpose because they were considered the same. . . .)

PE: Right. . . .

FP: They've been disregarded. In what way do you give a voice to vermin and slaves?

PE: I can recall when I started working on the stories the excitement of the challenge that most history is unknown. I wanted to find a way to what had never been recorded. I wasn't outside of the work enough to think "what an arrogant project!"

FP: It's not arrogant, it's necessary.

PE: It seemed necessary to me. I had this strong sense that most people in most times in most places have been illiterate. Even most people who've given testimony, who've written things—their words have not survived. Most history is gone; there's just a hole. We look at these walls [of Montolieu], we look at these stones, each one has a story but we could look at them a long time. In the end, you invent the story, you create the memory. And from inside the story-teller it feels as if you're listening to—say, a stone, and the stone has the voice of a Cathar[3] in it, or whomever, and you're giving the Cathar a voice.

FP: But why vermin in particular?

PE: In the case of the sugar plantation, the rats were terrible problems to the planters. This business of eating rats emerged in my researches—that they actually did. After a while, my character told me that he didn't want to eat rat. But also, I have to say that in an earlier draft of the story, Pierre didn't protest against eating rat. He was not so critical of his master's work. As I worked

---

3. The Cathars were a heretical Christian sect of the twelfth and thirteenth centuries that flourished in Southern France. They challenged the authority of the pope, who called a twenty-year-long crusade against them. At least 200,000 were killed.

with his story, he spoke to me more and more strongly about his sense of what had been left out. Actually I wasn't thinking of the arguments between social historians and king-and-general historians, but in a way, it is that argument.

FP: So you look at people's lives . . .

PE: . . . to try and imagine what their lives were like.

FP: To re-create them?

PE: Right. You might ask why I don't just do historical novels. But if I don't make it somehow strange for myself, if I don't make it mysterious, then I'm approaching history with a distance and confidence that people living in it could not have had. So I have to make it strange for myself in order to put myself in the position of a person who was living with the same sense of trying to figure it out that you or I would have. We can't see ourselves. We live our whole lives trying to figure out what our place is, what we're doing, what everyone around us is doing. You know, if you do a lot of research on the past, you say, "oh, *les Cathares* believed this and that—"

FP: —and it sounds so matter of fact. . . .

PE: It's matter of fact to us, but it wasn't to them.

FP: They were sorting it out.

PE: They were sorting it out. I like to write about something I'm sorting out along with the characters. I also don't want the burden of trying to tell stories that have to be true to facts that I can never know well enough.

FP: And in that way you are truer to facts. Here's another question I had: a critic says (about a part of your novel) that it's "what appears to be a historical novel." Would you subscribe to that?

PE: No, I wouldn't. It has historical elements, but so much is made up. The islands are made up, though the details of sugar production are pretty accurate. Nobody allowed a slave to learn to read and write in that culture, so Pierre's literacy is made up. And his longevity—there was a terrible turnover: a terrific death rate—actually among the Europeans as well. They had a hard time in the tropics. Actually, the French weren't as foolish as the English—English houses were thick-walled, and the early settlers wore dark, heavy clothes with ruffs. I took a few liberties with time too, by the way, between the era when people wore ruffs and went out in black—

FP: —gowns?

PE: Well, not gowns, but pantaloons, and jerkins, and when they wore waist-coats and breeches—the eighteenth century. The relationship that the master has with Buffon is not made up. That's a relationship that Buffon actually had with his *correspondants*. But many of the animals that they record are made up, the fish in the sea, for instance.

FP: What about the format, here, the title page: this really looks like a title page from the eighteenth-century tradition.

PE: That I wanted, right.

FP: What's important to you in this tradition?

PE: Well, this does purport to be the account of a slave telling about his life, and there are authentic slave narratives—you know Olaudah Equiano?

FP: Yes.

PE: Why does this period interest me? Well, Buffon was pre-enlightenment. So this is the moment in history when the urge to catalogue every thing, the encyclopedic urge, is present, but before the division of voices into vivid and precise. So there is observation and commitment to analysis but there's still that sense of enchantment, of the suffusion of the landscape with imagination. That moment appealed to me as a very full moment in human history. The French part of it—why he's not English—the English struck me as having been brutes in the new world. The English and the Dutch were these huge drunk-ards [laughter], the thoughtful Founding Fathers notwithstanding. When you learn basic history in American grammar schools, you learn that the Declaration of Independence is the ultimate enlightenment document, the ultimate promise of democracy and suffrage. I began to realize that our Declaration of Independence, for all I think it is beautifully written—and I can see why Ho Chi Minh liked it—the French Revolution was more thoroughgoing than our own, because it granted much more suffrage, it gave a greater voice to the common man. Toussaint L'Ouverture and the people that mounted the revolution in Haiti thought they were part of the French Revolution. And then Napoleon sent troops because France wanted the sugar revenues. The Haitians won their independence, but they were terribly betrayed. To me, what happened in Haiti was another great watershed in human history, like the division between the precise and the vivid voices, and perhaps related to it. I liked working with these twinned sets of ideas, and Buffon and Haiti—the only successful slave revolt—both pointed me to the French rather than the English colonial experience. I have to say also the challenge of creating an intellectual appealed to me. You know, there aren't many in literature—there's Hamlet, there's Brecht's Galileo. . . . I thought of creating in Pierre a great lost scientist, someone who'd had experiences that no one had had before, yet who came from a disregarded—there's the vermin!—a disregarded background. I hope the reader would become aware of what a range of lost opportunity for creativity and human development there is in the apartheid mentality that prevails even today.

FP: You picked the French colonization rather than the English—your fable world is also very foreign. In what way does your distancing help you see things differently?

PE: In the case of picking the French colonization, there is a fascination with French literature, although much of what I quote in the book is made up, I have to say—it's not only Le Montal, but other imaginary writers.—

FP: Such as? You said the cities were made up—

PE: In "The Hungry Girls"?

FP: They sound so French. . . .

PE: They're all made up. "Brosse-les-Bains"? [laughter] It's nonsense. "Anse-le-Marteau"—"Goose-the-Hammer"—it means nothing. "Parsee" (from the story "Snakeskins")—now that is an actual old word for Persian, but "Galub" is not an actual city. "Salah Dey Oum" is not that I know an actual name.

FP: But wait. "Goose-the-Hammer"—"Anse-le-Marteau"—anse does not mean "goose." Ole means "goose." Anse means "handle."

PE: Whoops! But you know, *ansérin* means "goose-like" in French and English (*anserine*). The Latin for "goose" is *anser*. Do you think a person who "fait le pot à deux anses" looks like a goose flapping its wings as well as a two-handled pot? "Handle-the-Hammer," "Goose-the-Hammer"—I can handle all those meanings! They goose the text and the reader.

FP: Is that what you had in mind?

PE: The answer is the anser.

FP: It's odd. "The Hungry Girls" sounds so French, the setting is so French—it's a mixture of what?—Flaubert, Maupassant?

PE: I guess I woke up here in Montolieu! [laughter]. "Kyono" [from the story "Milady's Ploy"] is a made-up place, but it's Japan-like. Li-Po was an eighth-century Chinese poet, but all these—"totojoni"—these are all made up.

FP: What about "The Change"? Everything is made up?

PE: "Hanewok," "Tongtu"—none of this exists. "Historian Veratius Aurelius" [from the story "Auravir"] did not exist. "Sophides" did not exist. There was one reviewer who accused me of stealing other people's history, which gave me a good laugh, because there's so much that's invented. I must have done something right if she thought that!

FP: What about the word-forging—that's made up too, of course—more made up than anything else. Here, in "Salt," for example, what about the "slukie"?

PE: I just liked the way it sounds—it sounds like the great silkie.

FP: What do you mean, "the great silkie"?

PE: "The Great Silkie of Sule Skerry" is a folksong—one of the ballads collected by Francis J. Child in *English and Scottish Popular Ballads*. "Slukie" is a little sideways skittle out of "silkie"—the way "Kyono" is a sideways scuttle from—there's just a lot of sideways motion in my stories.

FP: What is this Child ballad about?

PE: Well, it's not quite about my monster, it's about a seal. "Salt" is a very concept-driven story, actually. I was just imagining a human history in which gender wasn't with us from the beginning.

FP: Because there are only female protagonists.

PE: Right. So then "Salt" is about the emergence of gender. What inspired me was reading about the chromosomes. You know there's XX, and I was always taught that the male was XY, but recently I discovered that Y means absence of the X. So there's XX and then there's X-.

FP: Minus?

PE: Right, X(X-). I was looking to put that into a story.

FP: Reworking the scientific background into a broader mythical scope?

PE: I couldn't have said it better, and I wish I had! The made-up words come from—I just liked the sound of them.

FP: You work by sounds. . . .

PE: Yes. And this story has a sound that the others don't have. Kind of an Irish sound [reading from "Salt" with an Irish accent]: ". . . before the slukie drove us into the fire of air. Yet I have heard of thousands of galiven laying each two eggs on the beach come spring."

FP: It's almost like verse, now that you're reading it out loud.

PE: Well, this story has a certain rhythm.

FP: What about the "vollows"?

PE: "Vollow"—no diphthong. [Reading with an Irish accent] "We had to fight the gulls for vollow room. . . ." I like the roundness—it's like eggs, "vollow"— and it's also like "hollow" it's like a "vowel." But that's after the fact, I just liked the sound of "vollow."

FP: You say it's like "vowel." Your characters often hatch children or words indifferently. They hatch words like so many children, or they hatch children like so many words. Could you elaborate on that?

PE: Well, I'm someone whose children are words, so . . . I have that very personal sense of the world.

FP: There's one sentence I would have liked you to explain to me: the first sentence of "Salt." I think it's a beautiful first sentence, but it's probably the most puzzling as well to me: "You sit before me your heart a cup, and who am I to gainsay you drink?" First of all, who's the "you"? What kind of an audience are you calling up?

PE: I can actually see the storyteller: she's very old, very, very old, she has very long white hair, a long white dress, she's sitting in a little—you wouldn't even call it a hut—it's a lean-to of reeds by the sea. It's a great flat beach with the water going way in and way out—there are rocks, high rocks . . . you have to walk way, way out to get to this place—it's almost like Mont Saint Michel. But you're not in danger of being drowned, it's just a long walk. She's spinning, spinning, and "you" is I or whoever is coming to hear the story. This is her story.

FP: And we're sitting before her our "hearts a cup"—to drink from her words?

PE: There's a meta-narrator here, quoting the whole story. You see, the story is this old woman's talking, but the person who has come to hear is implied. "You" is a character in the story, then, who becomes the reader. Or the reader becomes the person who's come to hear.

FP: And when you say "who am I to gainsay you drink," we're drinking from her cup of words. . . .

PE: Well, the heart a cup is kind of a disgusting metaphor [laughter]. . . .

FP: What do you mean, disgusting?

PE: Disgusting in the way that Christian relics are disgusting. Parts of the body. . . . I grew up in the same town as (later) Madonna, "the material girl." Church and religion weren't very important to us. I did have Catholic friends who had cards in their wallets with these hearts like from an anatomy book—crowns of thorns around them. And these "sacred hearts" had veins in their pink muscle walls, maybe an artery or two poking out, and superimposed on the heart Christ crucified. There is a disconcerting literalness to the representation. One of the heresies of the Cathars was, they denied the humanity and the physicality of the suffering and resurrection of Christ. The "heart a cup" is disgusting in the same way then as certain familiar elements of orthodox Christianity.

FP: Are we drinking blood, or almost. . . .

PE: Well, if the heart's a cup and then the story is poured into the heart, there is certainly quite an explicit sacrificial element there. Now I'm talking after the fact, I didn't think about this when I wrote it. But if I have to say what it means, especially since it's the first sentence of a story of origins, then I have to acknowledge that it points to the sacrificial basis that Propp[4] has recognized in all story, although I hadn't read Propp when I wrote "Salt." But is this anybody in particular's blood? Well . . . let's just say this is a story about something being lost or sacrificed.

FP: And the mothers are sacrificed. Very often, in your fiction, the mothers are sacrificed when they give birth to words or children or eggs. . . .

---

4. Vladimir Propp (1895–1970) was a Soviet folklorist and scholar who analysed the basic structural elements of Russian folk tales to identify their simplest irreducible structural units. *Wikipedia: The Free Encyclopedia.* "Vladimir Propp," September 2019. http://en.wikipedia.org/wiki/Vladimir_Propp

PE: Well, you are a mother and you were just talking about not getting much sleep! I've just noticed that children eat up their parents' lives!

FP: That's right! And you make it so real.

PE: It's not something that people allow themselves to talk about much who have children—

FP: They block it out?

PE: Since I don't have them, I'm permitted to observe it. . . . [laughter]

FP: But what about intellectual creation, isn't that exhausting too? And don't you get out a lot more than you thought you would?

PE: I try not to think. I listen and I write by ear so as to block out judgment. I couldn't possibly write if I were thinking about all the things we're talking about. Thoughts—opinions about what I have done—are afterthoughts. The very notion of intellectual creation is much more abstract than the feel of the process—well, you're an intellectual yourself, so—

FP: But artistic creation is something else, it comes from a "deeper" level, it's not analyzed.

PE: True. And I had to learn not to analyze, or at least not to judge. The older I get, the better I understand that I come from quite a repressive background, although on the face of it, an indulgent American household. It certainly was not a family that encouraged—by contrast, if you think of [the proprietor] of the bed-and-breakfast, if you think of her creating it and making it into a work of art in the book village that her father had so much to do with founding— right away it's an unusual family where the generations are so comfortably and creatively involved with one another.

FP: So it's hers in the most deeply creative sense.

PE: The most deeply creative. She's not just running it, she's making something of it. It's a little hard for me to imagine that kind of a creativity in the family

context. I guess this speaks to that question you asked about filiation. It's been important for me as a woman to come to terms with this issue.

FP: Speaking of filiation—there is a story, and I can't pronounce the title—

PE: [Arabic accent] "R'ha-l'a R'a-H'oum[5]"!

FP: That sounds very Arabic! Where you say: "The elderly females swell to a tear-shape. Even as the pale, round eggs are sliding from their bodies, hatch-lings are gnawing at their shells. They will battle their siblings and charge the ranks. They will not look back." This idea of not looking back—

PE: This is really a pitiless story. . . .

FP: It is. It's a very harsh one.

PE: This is the harshest of all my stories. So little pity, I don't know what to say. We would like to think that people behave well in circumstances of scarcity, but they don't necessarily. There's a meanness to these people's lives, their phys-ical lives, but a certain grandeur in their religious conceptions. I don't know if I would call this any kind of emblem for my own mentality, but one thing really surprises me. That is the metaphysical element. When I read through these stories as a body of work, I see that there is a rather fierce metaphysical curiosity, an appetite, really, that has no place in my conscious life. I'm not a believer, but I am hungry to believe.

FP: Do you think being raised in a non-believers' household triggered your hunger?

PE: Maybe! In a certain way, it was a forbidden thing in the household I grew up in. Religion beyond knee-jerk pieties was not our family's way. Somebody's idea of rebellion might be to take a lot of cocaine—mine might be to flirt with religion.

FP: Something irrational that was not allowed, something suspiciously

---

5. *Conjunctions* 18: 1 (1992): 342.

looked at?

PE: Yes. It's a great luxury in a certain way. Certainly it's the only luxury (for the characters in the story "R'ha-l'a R'a-H'oum"). This is a tremendously sad story.

FP: But it deals with very important things; you can't read it and escape unharmed.

PE: There is hunger in the world at large. Scarcity. Pain. Cruelty. Suffering. I don't understand how people can say "you create these terrible worlds"—don't they read the newspapers? We live in islands of peace and plenty in France and the United States, don't you think?

FP: Of course. Look at where we are. . . . In your essay "Beaming Up: Liberal Arts and Literacy for the Next Century[6]," you mention "hortatory and didactic genres such as sermons, morality plays, fables, and parables which present the right-wrong polarities of manipulated obedience and which thus subvert the smarmy prescriptiveness of the [*Star Trek*] series and the global, open question that characterizes liberal studies: What does it mean to be human?" Obviously, you consider those forms—fables and parables—restrictive in a way. So why would you use them?

PE: They're teaching stories. Perhaps parables, inviting more multiple interpretation, don't quite belong in there.

FP: What about fables?

PE: Well, it's interesting—you know there's a new translation of Aesop. It seems the rigid little stories we know are nineteenth-century creations. The actual stories are much more like Jack stories, they're real survival stories, they're down-to-earth and really gritty. I think I need to qualify some of what I said about fables.

FP: You mean about the constraints of the fable?

---

6. *Central Park*, ed. Stephen-Paul Martin et al. No. 24 (Spring, 1995).

PE: Yes. Earlier, you asked about traditional forms and inscribed voices, the "pastiche" question. The truth is that I don't work in traditional forms. I work in re-invented traditional forms.

FP: Exactly. That's what I wanted you to get into.

PE: I'm always surprised when the word "pastiche" is used. I'm not sure of its derivation, but it reminds me of pasticcio, pasta, cookbooks. There would be something cynical and crafty about a writer who mixed a pinch of this and a pinch of that, cooked the whole mess—maybe not cynical, but certainly it would be an artisanal mentality, which, come to think of it, I may in fact possess! There is a prejudice nowadays against the idea of the work of art—art that is patently artificial, or artefactual. And it is true that trompe-l'oeil is an ancient tradition, mimesis, the representation of life—but so is tall tale. Anyway, supposing for the moment that I am a "mere" cook, let me give you a recipe for *The Hungry Girls*. An important ingredient is natural history, fermented by inversion, braised in hypothesis, seasoned with experimentation, a pinch of history, a pinch of anthropology, a dusting of oral tradition—a cup or two of sideways scuttle.

FP: What do you mean, "sideways scuttle"?

PE: Well, here we are in, let's say nineteenth-century France, or the France of Jean Giono or whomever, and bangety-boomer! A sideways scuttle into the France of the imagination. That's not much of a scuttle, though; it's a bigger one from Japan to Kyono. Never in Japan were there stags with these bizarre sexual habits (in "Milady's Ploy"); sleeve-dogs I believe were Chinese. A lot in that story is made up, but it echoes the courtly conventions, of say, Lady Murasaki's Japan.

FP: Some real anchorage, but yet—

PE: But yet it is invented. Lady Murasaki writes about people who were so discreet that they ate behind screens. They did not want to acknowledge any bodily functions.

FP: Is it only women, or is it men also?

PE: Women more than men, I recall, but that's a good question.

FP: So the concerns of Murasaki's characters are the opposite of your characters' usual concerns—her characters refuse to acknowledge bodily functions.

PE: That's the other side of the coin, isn't it? Maybe you were writing about sideways scuttles when you were writing about similes. I once read a very interesting article about the psychological processes that are inherent in certain figures of speech. I can't remember what they all were, but displacement is expressed, it seems, as metonymy. And there's a sense in which all fiction is metonymy or synecdoche. I let this piece of iron and this railing stand for the house—I can't possibly replicate the whole house, and anyway, it's not about that. If I want to give the reader Françoise, I'll give them your glasses or your ears. Maybe that process is carried a little further in my stories. It's just a thought, and some of what I thought you were getting at that in your article.[7]

FP: Thanks.

PE: It is by analogies and a cantilevering out from some known anchorage that in some ways I can—it's like an inchworm: here's the leaf and then he . . . but maybe my inchworm starts in the leaf and then anchors himself in the air and then goes from there. But he starts in the leaf.

FP: To go on and on.

PE: Right. That's what I mean by a sideways scuttle. But going back to the cookbook, the recipe, the list of ingredients—the civet may be seasoned in a few other ways too. One is—in many of the stories there's what I would call a voiceover voice—the narrator of Encyclopedia Britannica film strips I watched as a schoolchild. The film would always be rolling before the sound came up, so it would come on with a kind of whining growl into coherence. Rwhooooo . . . ! And then there'd be some music, and this deep, bland know-it-all voice would tell about the land and people of Indonesia. . . . Like God was talking. And that voice to a child, to me, was the voice of inescapable truth. So

---

7. "La comparaison en mue dans les nouvelles de Patricia Eakins," *Revue française d'études américaines* 73 (juin 1997): 14–21.

to give that voice to made-up things is to lend to invention the voice of veracity, of the unquestionable. Pseudologia. Playing around with that notion of the reliable omniscient narrator. Actually, my narrator isn't ever all that omniscient, because he knows he's in history, but he is sincere. In utter sincerity, the narrator gives you Brosse-Les-Bains and Le Montal. But the author's sincerity is suspect. She's having fun there, and maybe she shares with her narrators a sense of how arbitrary names are, how fragile a marker over the void, the black hole of history, the name of any village or any writer is.

FP: And so often the narrator is wondering about his own narration at the same time—

PE: As the author is lying—wondering and lying.

FP: Isn't that what fiction is all about?

PE: To tell a big lie that's true. Or a big lie that will somehow save you. When I was a child I read a lot of books where dogs and horses were the heroes. Children's pot-boilers—Albert Payson Terhune's books about collies and Anna Sewall's *Black Beauty*, about a wonderful horse. I think my imaginary animals continue in some ways from those hero dogs and horses, but without a child's—those books portrayed a world of right or wrong, whereas my stories portray a world in which that ideal has been betrayed.

FP: So that's a departure from the classical fable idea. And you twist around the framework of the fable to unsettle the certainty that is usually attached to it.

PE: Yes. But "unsettling certainty" sounds like serious subversion. I think there is just a lot of mischief in my stories. A playfulness that is a very direct continuation of childhood. For instance, one influence that I can see or hear in "The Hungry Girls" is—I had a record when I was a child, a phonograph record called "The Noisy Eater"—Jerry Lewis—I can't tell you how much I loved that record. I suppose children were given it so that they wouldn't grow up to go Krrrrunch . . . Grrrraw . . . Slooorp when they ate. But I loved all the noises Jerry Lewis made, it was horrible and wonderful. I don't have the record any more.

FP: But the memory of it is still very vivid.

PE: Yes. When the play (adapted from "The Hungry Girls") went up—last summer—it's going to be revived, by the way, August 19–30—for the program I had to say all my influences. I said Robert Coover, Italo Calvino, Borges, Ursula Le Guin—my grad-school mentor, George Chambers—I put all that in the program, but I didn't put Jerry Lewis and hero dog books, and they belonged there too.

FP: So the munching sounds—I mean the sounds—when you read your stories I can hear the sounds better. Was sound important to you?

PE: Very! There's a saying that the ear is the direct route to the heart, and that is true in the most literal way. You know, the ear is the only organ that receives the world directly into the body. We register "bird" with our eyes, but a bird doesn't fly into our brain. We register "bird song" with our ears, and the sound actually enters our brain and our body. But there was something else I wanted to say—about the idea of pastiche. That my work is not so much about inscribing a given writer's style—though I do some mimicry. I have been much more interested in creating stories that grow from the implications of basic distinctions in made-up cultures. So there really is quite a constructive process. I am not a big reader of Levi-Strauss—but what he describes about how cultures are built up in a series of oppositions is very analogous to the process by which I have built my stories— The stories accumulate gradually, often from some very small beginning. In the case of "Oono," I am quite sure the name came first. Then I made an animal to fit the name. Then I made people to say the name of the animal and to hunt him. Then I made the mythology of the people who hunt the animal.

Much of the writing I did in a house upstate that my husband was renovating. It was summer, the temperature on the second story of the uninsulated house rose each day to 100 degrees Fahrenheit, and while I worked with paper and pen, my husband was working with very noisy power tools. It is possible that the intensity of the story reflects in some measure the difficulty of concentrating on what I was writing under such conditions. I had to concentrate extra hard to compensate!

Later, while I was revising the story, I did do a lot of browsy reading in a very free-associational way, skipping around from one thing to another, seeing what caught my attention. Some of my reading was in popular natural history—*National Geographic* and *Natural History* magazines, which have lots of photographs. At some point I read a book called *Kabloona*, by Gontran de Poncins. I have read Jerome Rothenberg's collection of Native American poetry *Technicians of the Sacred*, which contains some Inuit poems and stories. I recall a museum exhibition of Inuit clothing and objects. Some dioramas of Inuit life at the Museum of Natural History. And I know I have seen the Robert Flaherty film [*Nanook of the North*, 1922].

Then there was a book I had as a small child, called *The Eskimo Twins*. This book gave me quite a vivid sense of Inuit customs and the Inuit way of life. The story was a simple adventure story that I have long forgotten. What stayed was that early, clear sense of the artifacts of Inuit life. It was from the implications of these artifacts, and of the animals, and of the basic features of the landscape, that I made up the mythology for the people I had invented.

But *The Eskimo Twins* also supplied the basis for a more performative understanding of Inuit life. My sister and I played a long-running freeform game based on the book. There is a sense in which the Ignook hunter of ooni in the kayak out on the sea in "Oono" is a little girl on an upside-down bridge table, paddling on the green-rug sea with a broom. The seal cooking over the fire is a milk-bottle seal. The sleeping shelves of "Oono" are the back stairs of our house, rising above a small vestibule that is the igloo. The babies on the shelves—a large collection of dolls wrapped in the hats and mufflers and jackets my sister and I would later wear outside to play.

Yet, my Ignook are not Inuit. When I wrote the stories that became *The Hungry Girls*, I made a conscious decision not to reflect any culture or known version of history in a completely accurate way. I wanted the sense of recognizable fragments joined with unrecognizable ones, but not for experimental purposes. And only a little to tease the reader. I wanted the stories to read as if the storyteller might always be on the verge of telling other stories. I wanted to create stories that read as if they came from the body of lost history. I had the sense, and have it now, that most of the history of most of the world has necessarily always been lost. And partly I wrote the stories to console myself for this loss, which I felt as a wound, a wound in the world, but also a personal wound, a loss as "original" to me as some people think sin is to mankind. A powerful sense of challenge and joy resides for me in the notion that there is a vast repository of untold story I can make and remake. To invent "the ignook" gave me a freedom that accurate ethnography would not have permitted.

FP: It's interesting that you have to bring in very different cultures from your own.

PE: Well, I may not always. I don't know why I started there, except I think there has always been something performative about my storytelling—as if the givens of a made-up cultural style were a costume or a skin and I were putting it on—a shaman's mask. I once saw a documentary about a Siberian shaman. She became possessed by her narrative powers after she went behind a simple curtain. She was in a room with a lot of other people, she went behind a curtain, she came back into the company in a mask that covered her head and was attached to a costume that fell all around her body. Inside her mask, her voice became the voice of the story. I think it is like that with me. Inside these masks I become the voices of the stories. However, there is quite a difference between my mask and that of the traditional shaman. The character of the traditional shaman's story was known to and shared by the culture of which the shaman was a part. There is a seamlessness, a unitariness, of culture and story. Whereas my mask is a multiple one formed of the fusion of a number of elements which are not all known to my readers or even to me and may not have been combined before, or not in this way. You could compare my narrative masks to Picasso's "Demoiselles d'Avignon." There is recognizable figuration there, the recognizable influence of African sculpture, but the point-of-view has been shattered. Sometimes the mask is the disembodied voice-over of Encyclopedia Britannica films, sometimes the voice is that of a wandering storyteller, sometimes the voice comes from within a culture, or from the border between cultures, as is the case with my character Pierre, who is first moved to tell the story of the African diaspora, and later moved to tell the story of his pregnancy, his hybrid children, and the culture he and his children share with underwater creatures he cannot completely know. Pierre sees himself as a trained observer, a savant in the European sense—after all he's a *correspondant* of Buffon—but he is also speaking from his own Africanness. And of course, he learns from his fishy "sons"—his unique experience—as well. But really, you were asking not so much "what kind of masks" as "why masks"? To hazard a guess—if you read my essay "Manifesto of a Dead Daughter"—the experience of marrying so much out of caste, of being disowned and hearing yourself pronounced dead—it changes your sense of yourself and your culture. You no longer see things the same way.

FP: And yet you still have the same history.

PE: Yes, but you don't know what to make of your own history. I have no objection to claiming it, nor am I ashamed of what my experience has been, but it has been very hard to speak of it. And being unable to speak is a kind of living death for a writer. But perhaps I felt somehow trapped in my culture, as if it were a coffin, I buried alive in it, all along.

Even as a small child growing up in a subdivision, I felt stifled by the narrow range of permitted culture, and there was a lot that I couldn't make sense of. One thing, for instance, that never occurred to me as a child, and that certainly occurs to me now, is the number of houses that had white pillars, they looked like southern slave-owners' houses, and this was in Michigan. And sometimes people even had those black iron jockeys up front with rings in their hands, fake horse-hitching posts. What were they thinking of themselves as?

FP: Plantation owners.

PE: Yes. And the Barthian sense of mythology really applies: here's this architectural style that's been borrowed to say something about these people. Here are all these children of immigrants and Okies, people risen from the working classes, who wanted to represent themselves as slave owners of the antebellum South. Marrying a Black ex-jailbird poet very young—I found myself so at odds with the subdivision culture of the Midwest, that I no longer felt at home in my own history. It was lost to me, and I began looking everywhere for it. I think you can read in those stories a quest or a search for the buried life of the "dead" writer, an obsession with transformation and birth. When I was writing "The Hungry Girls" I was very conscious of trying to revive buried or find lost stories, though when I was writing I saw these excavations as archaeological expeditions into the collective unconsciousness.

FP: And yet we still have to face our own history.

PE: Yes. It's buried in my stories somehow. I won't say coded because I don't think I have any sense of hiding.

FP: You would have conformed if you had hidden.

PE: That's right.

FP: To me, this is very coherent with your work.

PE: Really?

FP: What you were saying about the masks. When a mask enables you to say so much more—

PE: I think that my masks helped me to speak from silence. Now whether everything I write will always be from masks, I don't know. What I'm working on now—

FP: I was curious about that. . . .

PE: I don't want to say too much about it because it's in process, but I'm interested in the Catskills where our house is, in the history of that region and the kinds of voices that naturally emerge from it. So that's a little closer to home.

FP: What about the book *Pierre*[8]. . . .

PE: It's a novel. It's not yet a book.

FP: How long a novel is it?

PE: Maybe 300 and some pages.

FP: Did you find it very different to work on a longer form than the short story?

PE: So much time and research went into creating the world of each story that in some ways I was already writing novels.

FP: But yet you chose to develop this one rather than the others.

---

8. *The Marvelous Adventures of Pierre Baptiste, Father and Mother, First and Last* (New York, New York University Press, 1999).

PE: Maybe if I weren't an ignorant autodidact, a depressive who sleepwalked through all her education, I wouldn't have to recreate the history of narrative, if you know what I mean. It's something I had to do for myself, to try on the whole history of narrative that Propp lays out. *Pierre* begins to explore the consciousness of the individuated hero, the hero of the bourgeois novel, although I didn't think that when I was writing the novel. I am not a salmon spawning my way to the mainstream, I'm just recapitulating—they say ontogeny recapitulates phylogeny.[9] What I think that means, in the womb, say, Armance (FP's baby) was like earlier forms of life before she was born—

FP: Like a fish—

PE: Like a fish or whatever. . . . I think it is the same thing for me as a writer. I am recapitulating the phylogeny of narrative. I can't say anything more about it. Shall we go for a coffee?

---

9. Ernst Heinrich Haeckel (1834–1919) enunciated the biogenetic law that in the development of the individual animal the stages through which the species has passed in the course of its historic evolution are repeated. He was the first to draw up a genealogical tree relating the various orders of animals. *Webster's Biographical Dictionary* (Springfield, Mass.: G & C. Merriam Co., 1959).

HERE BE DRAGONS

A CONVERSATION WITH JEFFREY MILLER, ORIGINAL PUBLISHER OF *THE HUNGRY GIRLS*, CADMUS EDITIONS

John Richards

Jeffrey Miller and writer John Richards sat down to revisit The Hungry Girls *in Jeffrey's Berkeley, California, apartment on the 30th anniversary of the book's original release. Cadmus Editions is a small, literary press in the Bay Area, whose many distinguished publications include Tom Clark's* The Great Naropa Poetry Wars, *Paul Bowles's* She Woke Me Up So I Killed Her, *as well as works by Federico García Lorca, William Burroughs and Gustaf Sobin, and many others. Friend and longtime correspondent of Patricia Eakins, John Richards is author of two novels, and a story collection,* The Pigeon Factory, *from Cadmus Editions.*

JEFFREY MILLER: Even though you forewarned me when you made the introduction to Patricia, that her work would upend my world, I was nevertheless entirely unprepared for *The Hungry Girls*, a manuscript of such elegant and confounding brilliance that I was struck dumb upon first reading it.

JOHN RICHARDS: I can't tell you how happy that made me. Back when Patricia and I were first exchanging stories, I hoped one day to write something as good as any one of these tales that became *The Hungry Girls*. When she eventually sent the whole manuscript my way, I sent it to you praying you would experience it the same way I did, and need to make it a book.

JM: I am immensely proud to have been *The Hungry Girls*'s publisher.

JR: Now thirty years after Cadmus Editions first sent *The Hungry Girls* into the world to wander on its own, who would have predicted meeting again to talk about the miracle of that book?

JM: Me. I would have. Yes, definitely. I understood immediately that in a literary sense, *The Hungry Girls* was news, a significant event. It was as if someone had sent me *The Voynich Manuscript* deciphered, decrypted, translated into elaborate English, or better yet, as if some newly discovered fabulist from the ages had written a bestiary . . . that resonated on previously unheard levels, tonalities. . . .

JR: Nice. *The Hungry Girls* evokes for you *The Voynich Manuscript*, a book hundreds of years old in an unknown script that has been waiting to be decoded . . . as if Patricia unlocked something in *The Hungry Girls* that has somehow existed forever, but yet has not been seen or understood before. . . .

JM: I can say when I first read *The Hungry Girls*, I was both bowled over and simultaneously deeply puzzled; the book's first impact was overwhelming, as a tour de force, as an artistic triumph of both necessity and mystery. For the life of me I couldn't articulate in a rational manner the huge response reading it worked on me, and the mystery abides.

JR: So it arrived on your doorstep. Among the hundreds of submissions you have had, and you, a small press publisher with no committee of readers, no group of other editors at your disposal, found what you were looking for here . . . what were you looking for?

JM: What I diligently look for are texts which contribute to humane discourse, add to the world of letters, add to the sum total of human knowledge.

JR: That doesn't sound like a publisher's marketing plan. It sounds more like a mission.

JM: I suppose it is. I don't publish to serve genres or sales goals or political fashions. I search for texts which have such stylistic niceties that reading them can modify the reader, perhaps subtly contribute to the humanity of the reader, and too, both please and amuse. . . .

JR: And what was it like to discover *The Hungry Girls*. . . .

JM: It was accompanied with that rush of excitement, adrenalin, hands trembling, saying out loud, "This is it!" . . . I had stumbled upon human treasure, palpable culture, the iterations of a voice transcribed, talent deserving the blessing of being replicated and sent forth as a printed book. Publishing is a world of ineffable mysteries. . . . I have no hard and fast rules, rather I react to delicate gradations of sensibility, aesthetics and have a willingness to put into print texts that are controversial, adversarial, contentious . . . sending forth hellfire and brimstone, and too, the breathtakingly beautiful.

JR: Which is *The Hungry Girls*?

JM: All of it. Elective affinities! Alchemical magic! Stylistic mastery, tone, brio, wit and profundity . . . for the purpose of creating such stonking, vibrating, copulating creatures in this endlessly complex bestiary.

JR: John Williams (author of *Stoner*) spent his career teaching at a university and writing novels, and insisted that works of art should not be analyzed, but experienced. It is the raw imaginative engagement with the work that makes the reading alter your genes and chromosomes, your DNA. I think what we keep describing is *The Hungry Girls* as an original experience, something wholly different. And yet I keep looking for its antecedents. When I asked Patricia what she was reading when she wrote the book she very modestly said, "The same as everyone else, I suppose, at the time, Borges, Calvino, García Márquez, Robert Coover, particularly *Pricksongs and Descants*," then she tagged on, a little impishly, I think, "Oh, and *National Geographic*."

JM: Her work is sui generis and so this question never occurred to me, so original, without obvious antecedents. I suppose you could suggest, Montaigne, Thomas Hobbes, Daniel Defoe. . . .

JR: Patricia's novel, *The Marvelous Adventures of Pierre Baptiste* is the *Robinson Crusoe* Dafoe wishes he had written. . . .

JM: I'm sure *The Hungry Girls* had François Rabelais rolling in his grave, clapping his hands and howling with delight! Not to mention Thomas More,

Jonathan Swift, La Fontaine, Mary Shelley, Jules Verne, William Blake, Edgar Allan Poe, putting their arms around her shoulders, waving her into the Pantheon. . . .

JR: Flaubert, Balzac, Twain. . . .

JM: And Darwin!

JR: I bet she read *Origin* . . . and his studies of earth worms. . . .

JM: Especially the worms! We could list dozens more and still miss those writers who most influenced her and the writing of *The Hungry Girls*. I'm certain, unlike many of us, her reading was as omnivorous and wide-ranging . . . as the creatures she dreamed up. I've wondered who were her teachers, where did she come from. . . .

JR: She was from polite Detroit, I was from impolite Detroit, in a time of decline and escape. I'm sure we both thought of ourselves as ships deserting a sinking rat. She moved to New York, I split for San Francisco, but we didn't meet till long after that.

JM: What brought you together?

JR: Prolific and important poet and teacher Faye Kicknosway, who insisted we enter our work listening to voices, seeing objects, connecting the unlikely . . . she suggested we should exchange letters and we discovered we shared a lot. We were swimming in the zeitgeist of the '60s and '70s. Question every-thing, seek always, embrace your ignorance, allow your imagination to show you the way.

JM: Truly an age of disruption.

JR: We were seeking new forms, new ways to say things, and that showed up in Patricia's work and my work. We are very different writers, but at our best, we embrace the freedom of a jazz composition, the work reveals itself in the doing. And we are both attracted to the extravagantly imagined . . . meanwhile, there you were in San Francisco. . . .

JM: Also committed to changing the status quo. When friends asked me to come down to some protest or demonstration, I could not because I was making books, a task I thought of, to paraphrase the Austrian painter Hundertwasser, as a revolution that required patience, "like dripping water on stone," that required my undivided attention. . . .

JR: And is the necessary link to complete the process Patricia begins with her work.

JM: I think of it as something much more important than just a responsibility. . . .

JR: When I talk to Patricia, she speaks to such simple triggers for these stories, for example, if animals eat their young, what if people did, too? And she is off and running. Every story a tale of strange transformation. She was laughing when she told me that she probably has so much psychological repression that the only way she could possibly free herself is in the disguise of these mythic fables.

JM: She speaks with such passion and clarity in her stories, I have no doubt they are brought into the light from some deep-rooted and intensely resonant place within her.

JR: In that same conversation she said that she understands that each story in some way is autobiographical . . . but that she often doesn't know *how* until long after she writes it.

JM: I'm not surprised. I think it is not unusual for an artist of such profound and intuitive gifts to fail to perceive her own depths.

JR: I recall Robert Frost's wily take on the question, something like, "If you found it in the poem, I intended it."

JM: Clever. But there is no question that Patricia draws upon cultural and literary history from around the globe: 19th-century France; medieval Persia, Lady Murasaki's 10th-century Kyoto; a post-Hiroshima and Nagasaki world located on a Pacific island radioactively polluted from bomb testing;

a Rome contemporaneous with Pliny the Younger and Greek antiquity . . . she even evokes the American frontier, not to say, realms seemingly entirely fictional as in her story, "Salt," which had me considering trade routes from Morocco to western Africa, camel caravans, North African Islamic kingdoms, even if the setting is ostensibly a mythic North . . . she dips into the Age of Exploration and the Age of Colonialism.

JR: You're on to her, I think. She has said to me that she always loved travel tales, explorer's journals, the strange, wondrous things she finds in nature, the surprising ways human beings interpret it all in their mythologies. . . .

JM: But finally, the question of where her thoughts have ranged is not important. What is important is that she, Patricia Eakins, managed to bring such treasure back across all the frontiers, lazzaretti, customs inspections . . . a great and crafty smuggler from the many beyonds . . . these acts of utter necessity and genius brought against all odds across all known barriers. Patricia, the fabulist, the fabricator, breathes life into those realms in medieval maps noted only as terra incognita . . . those uncharted regions bearing the ominous legend and watchword, "Here Be Dragons."

JR: Recently I spent an afternoon with Patricia and her husband, poet and memoirist, Peter Martin, at the Dia:Beacon in New York. It was fascinating to be with them. As we moved past David Heizer's monumental stones, Chamberlain's twisted metal, the leaning sheets of Richard Serra's iron bearing down on us, each new work was a revelation that drew gasps from the two of them. I was so taken with Patricia's total, visceral, even preverbal engagement with the art we were viewing. It was as if, through her own unfiltered experience of the art, she was drawing back curtains and throwing open windows for me . . . that freshness, that wonder infuses her writing. That's how I think of her. . . . How was she to work with?

JM: A great pleasure. . . . We worked very closely together. I once likened it to a couplet from Ed Dorn, "They go together/Like marble steps and fancy dancers." Patricia is very funny; she has a sly, glancing, slightly off-center sense of humor . . . and *The Hungry Girls*, among its many, many virtues, is a very, very funny book.

JR: Such an unusual book, were you worried about its reception, whether it would find an audience?

JM: I never, ever try to answer this craft/trade question. Rather, I believe that important work finds its audience, through word of mouth, the mystical circulation of objects in the universe. Cadmus Editions has always teetered on the razor's edge. Every book ventured, published, is a risk, a great risk, but this is what a literary publisher does, endeavors, magicks works into print and then, *publicare*, sends them forth. But the reception of this work was exceptional, from the many well-known and prestigious authors who stepped up even before the finished book saw light of day. . . .

JR: And how did it do when it did show up on shelves?

JM: Patricia is one of the hardest working authors I have ever encountered. The first edition sold out because she tirelessly promoted it, gave so very many readings. She would, I believe, accept any venue's invitation to read and sell books that sated the hunger (forgive the pun) that her reading had just created. Extraordinary grit, perseverance, toughness.

JR: Any disappointments?

JM: Yes, one big one. I thought when the first edition was expended, this edition from a small, marginal literary press on the West Coast would be quickly picked up by a major press, which would have the resources and heft to promote it to a larger, wider audience . . . but that never came to pass. I am therefore very grateful to Rick Schober and Tough Poets Press for doing the honors on the 30th anniversary of its original production.

JR: Did *The Hungry Girls* require editing, or did it arrive fully groomed and realized?

JM: Like everything about Patricia, her work arrived in impeccable form, shape . . . and I do not believe I so much as changed a single comma or period. It was immediately clear that I was in the presence of a master of prose . . . an acute intelligence . . . a perfectionist.

JR: *The Hungry Girls* is as powerful and relevant today as the day it was written.

JM: It's timeless, for today, and for posterity. I simply count my blessings, that I had the honor of sending it forth into the maelstrom of life.

JR: A bit unfair if you ask me.

JM: How so?

JR: Patricia gets to live forever with this work, and meanwhile, if we're lucky we'll be tagged on as a footnote.

JM: That's the way it goes, isn't it?

JR: I suppose we could be tagged to worse things.

JM: Mass murder. . . .

JR: Corporate malfeasance. . . .

JM: Well, we'll always have Patricia.

JR: Yes . . . and that's not so bad . . . and she will say, they were "last seen as an eddy of dust on the road."

THE HUNGRY GIRLS: A FAIRY TALE

A WORK OF MOVEMENT THEATRE

Stephanie Gilman and Kristin Tanzer of Collision Theory (formerly girl &
co) were co-creators—adaptors and producers—of The Hungry Girls: A Fairy
Tale. *Stephanie Gilman directed; Kristin Tanzer was choreographer and a*
principal performer. The show premiered at Synchronicity Space, in New York
City, in August 1997. There was a revival in August 1998 as part of the New
York International Fringe Festival.

The Hungry Girls! How thrilled, enthralled, devastated, startled and ultimately excited I was to read this story. I was introduced to the stunning
piece by a friend at Oberlin College in the '80s. Our plan was to make a giant
puppet adaption. Although that never came to fruition, the story came back
into my life when the theater company I co-ran, Collision Theory, was looking for material and inspiration. We created highly stylized physical theater,
and "The Hungry Girls" was a perfect fit.

It is a massive understatement to say the story is theatrical and visual.
What made it so perfect for us, is that it also lent itself to performance by a
large ensemble, to a heightened sensibility, and to the mythic and epic states
we were so drawn to as theater artists. We somehow found a way to contact
Patricia Eakins (this was 1996–1997, so before the Internet!), and it was the
beginning of a beautiful, creative collaboration. Patricia was tremendously
generous with her story and her time, and supported us throughout the process of bringing *The Hungry Girls* to life. We wanted to make sure we honored her vision and imagination, while making something that would work
as theater.

We produced the first incarnation of the show at the now defunct Synchronicity Space in Soho, and the second production was at the New York
International Fringe Festival. I can still see images from the show in my

All photos © Dixie Sheridan.
Collision Theory, NYC Fringe, 1998

head, and hear Patricia's words . . . the funny, and ultimately very sad story of Jeanne and all the hungry girls. It is certainly an experience, and a story, I will never forget.

—*Stephanie Gilman*

Part of the challenge and thrill of working on the theatrical adaptation of *The Hungry Girls* was discovering how to best engage with Patricia's use of language. As her readers know, Patricia's work is not only rich in imagery and narrative, the words themselves have their own character. They demand to be spoken. They have a feel in the mouth when said aloud.

With the ensemble, we set out to find the movement and physical language of the piece as it related to the text. Looking back, there were three essential ways we used the text: putting it center stage to stand on its own, moving with the text, and moving in place of the text.

When Particia's words stood alone, the theatrical elements served as a container or scaffold. We used a relatively simple movement vocabulary: a single gesture, a tension-filled walk across the stage, a tableau, stillness. In these moments, the actors spoke and we let the words hang there, reverberating in the space. For example, the haunting refrain, "If only she were a lunatic to be chained to her bed and forgotten. But she is not crazy. Only hungry."

When we moved with the text, we let the rhythms and tempos inherent in her use of language fully inform our choices. The villagers' scenes are a perfect example. The actors' movements created a physical expression of the characters' outrage, disgust, and eventual hatred. Their movements were quick, forceful, menacing. Their bodies struck with the same force as the language.

Finally, when we used movement in place of or in the spirit of the text, we embodied the less tangible elements. The atmospheric, visceral, and emotional scope of the text. We moved scarcity, gluttony, greed, madness . . . and, of course, the enormity of the girls' bodies, hunger and desire.

Working on *The Hungry Girls* with Patricia was an expansive professional experience, which to this day, still influences my life and work.

—*Kristin Tanzer*

Poster for *The Hungry Girls: A Fairy Tale* signed by members of the cast.

THE HUNGRY GIRLS NIGHTDRESSES

MIXED MEDIA FIBER ARTWORK BY MOIRA BATEMAN

"The Hungry Girls Nightdress No. 7" (linen textile, onion skin dye, raw wool, wood and metal yoke) by Moira Bateman. Photo by Peter Lee.

I think of *The Hungry Girls* as an important influence for me as an artist. Before I read the story, I attended a performance of its adaptation to see my good friend, Kathy Hendrickson, in the New York Fringe Festival in 1998. As I was five months pregnant with my first child, I was especially mesmerized by the wild language and imagery that related to giant women and pregnancy, child bearing, voracious appetites and dirt eating. The story felt very elemental to me and seemed to strike at something intrinsic to instinctual human nature. Ideas from this story have resurfaced in my artwork as I look back twenty-one years later. The most obvious influence is on my series of wild, large-scale linen and raw wool giantess nightdresses inspired by the one nightgown the hungry girls fought over. The dresses I made represented the girls themselves, and often featured large abdominal holes or cuts with stitching and mending. The large dresses were the beginning of my work in textiles as well as instrumental in my shift from outdoor and landscape-based work to gallery work and my current mud-dye and waxed cloth abstractions.

—*Moira Bateman*

ABOUT THE AUTHOR

© Tatiana Daubek Photography

Patricia Eakins is the author of *The Hungry Girls and Other Stories* and *The Marvelous Adventures of Pierre Baptiste* (a novel) which won both the NYU Press Prize for Fiction and the Capricorn Fiction Award of the Writer's Voice. Her work has appeared in *The Iowa Review, Parnassus, Conjunctions,* and *The Paris Review,* which awarded her the Aga Khan Prize for Fiction.

Eakins has been awarded two creative writing fellowships from the National Endowment for the Arts, one from NYFA, one from CAPS, and the Charles Angoff Award from *The Literary Review.* She was a 2010 honoree of the Uptown Art Stroll for her excellence as curator of the Sunday Best Reading series in Northern Manhattan.

In 1997, "The Hungry Girls" was made into a work of theatre by the performance ensemble Collision Theory, which later commissioned Eakins to write the texts and lyrics for *Portrait (with horse and other).* These texts appear in the Artist in Wartime Issue of *Fiction International* under the title "What Remained."

Eakins is the subject of *Reading Patricia Eakins,* a book of critical studies of her work edited by Françoise Palleau, who has also translated *The Hungry Girls* into French (*Les Affamées,* University of Grenoble Press, 2010).

ACKNOWLEDGMENTS

Profound thanks are extended to the following for their generous financial support which helped to defray some of this book's production costs:

Kevin Adams, Bulent and Olga Akman, Zynab Hashim Al-Ma'Ali Tabatabaei, Matt Armstrong, Katrin Artner, Ash, Eloise Ruth Auld, Thomas Young Barmore Jr, Matthew Beckham, Cameron Bennett, Matthew Boe, Timothy Bohman, Matt Bucher, Myla Calhoun, Jeffrey Canino, Tim and LeeAnne Carlson, Hannah Carroll, Tobias Carroll, April J Chase, Scott Chiddister, Alexander Cobb, C. Colla, Joshua Lee Cooper, Sheri Costa, Thad DeVassie, Linda Dunne, Isaac Ehrlich, Steven Elsberry, Pops Feibel, Meghan Fredrich, Thomas Fuchs, Nathan "N.R." Gaddis, GmarkC, Brenda Goodman (brendagoodman.com), Natalie Grand, Elizabeth Charlotte Grant, Mark Greeley, Douglas Gunnarsson, André H., Erik Hemming, Aric Herzog, Per Kristian Hoff, Melissa Hooper, Shannon Horton, Erik T Johnson, Griffin Irvine, Brian C Jones, Hernán Julin, Haya K., Handsome Ryan Kennedy, Atticus Lanigan, Don La Rocca, Otto Lindgren, Gardner Linn, T.B. Lucas, Peter Martin, Donna Lorelei Mason, Marci McCann, Sidney McMahon, Stephanie Meade, Dr. Melvin "Steve" Mesophagus, Andrew Miazga, Mark Molnar, Jonathan Morton, Geoffrey Moses, Gregory Moses, Séamus Murphy, J.W. Dionysius Nicolello, Elizabeth Norman and Gwyn Zeeck, Richard Ohnemus, Michael O'Shaughnessy, Danny Paige, Ry Pickard, K.L. Pinkoski, Poems-For-All, Pedro Ponce, Borys Pugacz-Muraszkiewicz, John Richards, Jennifer Riel, Nichole Robertson, Roxanne, Sebastián Riquelme Sáez, George Salis, Frank V. Saltarelli, Kristen Scanlan, Spike Schwab, Susan Sermoneta, Sean Stewart, Anderson Todd, Paul and Laura Trinies, Anna Truwe, Cato Vandrare, Adam Virnelson, Jack Waters, Christopher Wheeling, Isaiah Whisner, Dan Wickett, Karl Wieser, Todd Wolfe, Andrew Wright, Liz York, The Zemenides Family, and Anonymous

CPSIA information can be obtained
at www.ICGtesting.com
Printed in the USA
FFHW012253241119
56112468-62205FF